THE CUP AND THE LIP

Journalist Peter Harkness had agreed to attend a literary brains trust in the place of Daniel Braile, a distinguished novelist who believed he was being poisoned. Was this an invalid's fancy or the truth? Whilst most members of Braile's household were attending the event, the aged author left his sick-room and disappeared without trace in the pouring rain. The group were at first reluctant to inform the police, but as the evidence pointed towards a horrifying conclusion, their united front cracked. Harkness discovered they were in fact deeply divided. It was not his only discovery...

THE CUP AND THE LIP

by
Elizabeth Ferrars

Magna Large Print Books
Long Preston, North Yorkshire,
England.

British Library Cataloguing in Publication Data.

Ferrars, Elizabeth
    The cup and the lip.

    A catalogue record for this book is
    available from the British Library

    ISBN 0-7505-1203-2

First published in Great Britain by William Collins Sons &
Co., Ltd., 1975

Copyright © 1975 by M.D. Brown

Cover photography by arrangement with The Last Resort
Picture Library

The right of Elizabeth Ferrars to be identified as the author
of this work has been asserted by her in accordance with
the Copyright, Designs and Patents Act, 1988

Published in Large Print 1998 by arrangement with Professor
Robert Brown by Power of Attorney

Magna Large Print is an imprint of
Library Magna Books Ltd.
Printed and bound in Great Britain by
T.J. International Ltd., Cornwall, PL28 8RW.

CHAPTER I

The argument that the telephone interrupted had been about violence.

It had been a comfortable argument, the kind that can go on for an evening, punctuated by digressions, by laughter, by the necessity to top up drinks, that can seldom be achieved except between old friends.

Max Rowley and Peter Harkness were very old friends. They had been at school together. A very minor public school, and a part of their friendship had grown out of the fact that they had hated it almost equally. Then they had gone to Oxford together, Max to study Law and Peter Medieval History. Then for a time their paths had diverged. Peter sometimes wondered why this had happened. Why had they drifted apart? Had it been, on his side, that for a time he had needed to escape from the dominance of Max's sharp, critical intellect? However, when they had met again accidentally on the Underground, their friendship had been casually resumed at the point, it seemed, where it had broken off.

Yet both of them had changed a great deal in the intervening years. Peter as a boy had been excessively shy, full of embarrassed consciousness of his oversized hands and feet, which had indicated that he would later be a big man, and had been charged with intense emotions which had caused him great suffering since he had not known how to express them. But with time he had acquired considerable confidence in himself and cared very little what others thought of him. Max, on the other hand, had become dignified and wary, a man who thought carefully before he spoke. He was married and lived in a block of flats near Regent's Park. He had become a partner in a firm of solicitors. Peter was still single, but close to trying to discover what a girl called Caroline might think about marriage, since it seemed the logical consummation of a surprisingly long-lasting relationship. He lived in a mews flat in Paddington, was a freelance journalist and writer of popular history and was generally worried about money.

On the cold March evening that he and Max spent together and somehow got into an argument about violence, both men had had to admit that, being too young to have been in the war, they had never encountered it personally, except in its twisted mental forms, since their schooldays. But both had encountered it then, though their experience of it had been singularly different. Max, a small boy with a clear brain and a long memory, had submitted to brutality with self-contained, unforgiving bitterness, waiting for the time when his cleverness would help him to achieve some revenge. Peter, who had been larger and with a temper that could be terrifying, once it blazed out of control, had retaliated to bullying with a ferocity that had scared his attackers. But this had not earned him respect. There had been something too emotional in his furies to seem proper to the conventional young, whom he frightened and who did not forgive him for it. And he had become afraid himself of his rages and at the back of his mind, now aged forty, he was still afraid of them.

This had left him with the conviction that violence is an inborn, horrifying evil, to be suppressed at all costs. Max, on the other hand, contended that if childhood could be happy and free from fear, the young were not naturally violent but had it instilled into them by the unpleasant example of their elders. Peter called this sentimentality and told Max that the trouble about him was that he simply did not dare face the existence in himself of the violence that was certainly there.

'Of course it's there in all of us, don't tell me it isn't,' Peter said. 'We enjoy hating, we enjoy cruelty, we enjoy destruction, even the least perverted of us. Would war have remained an honoured institution in our society for all these aeons if we hadn't a natural love of it? And what's ever had the slightest

8

effect in controlling that obscene love but fear?'

'There you go again—fear!' Max exclaimed. 'How you keep harping on it. What is it you're so afraid of, Peter?'

'Of myself, of myself!' Peter answered. 'Haven't I been telling you so for the last hour? And if you aren't afraid of yourself too, God help you! That sort of fear's a great safeguard, d'you know that? Now tell me, aren't you a little afraid of yourself? Inside that nicely balanced brain of yours, isn't there a trace of irrational fear of what you might do, given the circumstances?'

'What circumstances, for instance?'

'I don't know. I don't know what your fatal temptation might be. And of course I don't expect you to tell me about it, even if you know what it is. Our fears are strictly private things. We've all got the right to try to conceal them.'

'The fatal temptation for me,' Max said thoughtfully, 'is most likely to be my clients' cash. I'm very attracted by money. You don't know how I'd love to find a safe way of getting some to stick to my fingers, after which I'd slip quietly off to South America. But violence, murder—which is what we're talking about, isn't it?—isn't a thing I'm much afraid of. Quite simply, I'm too squeamish. You know me well enough for that. I'm not sure if I'm what you'd call afraid of myself, but I do know I'm a physical coward. I don't care much for the sight of blood. I dislike the feeling of firearms. But of course I'm interested in the subject in the abstract. I mean, if one isn't somehow attracted by it, as you say, why does one listen to the nine o'clock news? I'm inclined to think that perhaps we actually sleep better after our regular dose of shootings and bombings and hijackings and rioting. So up to that point I agree with you. And d'you know, I've sometimes thought I'd like to know a murderer. Oddly enough too, a murderer who'd committed some particularly atrocious sort of crime.'

It was then that the telephone rang.

Max got up to answer it. He was host that evening. They were in the Regent's Park flat. Max's wife, Kate, was away, staying with friends. The room that they were in, not a very large one, was cluttered with too much furniture for comfort, with a dining table and sideboard at one end and a number of easy chairs at the other, gathered around the gas fire, and with bookcases round the walls, reaching from floor to ceiling. The room in the flat that had been intended as a dining-room had been taken over by Kate, who was a novelist and needed somewhere to work. In the crowded living-room Peter always felt as if he were too large and too clumsy to have been allowed loose in it.

He was in fact a large man, but not clumsy. His big, knuckly hands were delicate in their touch and the movements of his wide-shouldered body were smooth and assured. He had sandy-coloured hair, thick and rough, and the wide, mild grey eyes that gave a face a look of innocent curiosity, even when this has very little to do with their owner's state of mind. His face was long, bony and ruddy and he smiled easily, though when there was no one there to see him his features had a way of settling into an expression of inward-looking melancholy.

Max, threading his way between the close-standing chairs to the telephone, was smaller, neater, in all ways more sharply defined. He was slender and fine-boned, with a calm, oval face, smooth dark hair and dark, observant eyes. In a slightly sombre way, he was extremely handsome. He dressed with great neatness and, as Peter knew, always looked after his clothes himself, because Kate's slap-happy way with them would never have kept them up to Max's standards.

He looked more than the forty that he was, but according to Peter's memory of him he had always had a middle-aged look, although he never seemed noticeably to age. It was as if, early in his life, he had found a mould that suited him and had decided to maintain it. In ten years' time he would probably look no older than he did at present.

'Yes?' he said into the telephone. 'Oh?... Oh yes, darling.'

He cupped his hand over the mouthpiece

and said to Peter, 'It's Kate.'

'Well, I'm glad you're enjoying yourself,' he went on.

A pause.

'Yes, he's here. You want to speak to him?' He turned to Peter. 'Kate wants to speak to you.'

He held out the telephone.

Peter rose and took it from him. He knew that Kate was staying at the home of Daniel Braile, an elderly novelist who just then exerted a great deal of influence over her and who lived in a great Victorian box of a house called Grey Gables near the small town of Sisslebridge.

He said, 'Hallo, Kate, how are you?'

'In a hole, Peter dear, a fearful hole,' she answered. Her voice was rather gruff, with a throaty sort of charm. 'I've been ringing you at your home all the evening and I tried Caroline's number too, but she didn't know where you were. Then I suddenly thought you might be with Max, so I tried our own number. I'm so glad I've found you. I want you to help me. I can count on you, can't I?'

'Of course—well, it depends.'

Peter thought that she probably wanted him to find some piece of information that she needed for the book on which she was working and that this would mean a trip to some museum or library, for which he had very little time at the moment. But for some reason Kate, though herself a writer, never thought of him as busy at all, because he did not work from nine till five, like her husband.

'Listen,' she hurried on, 'you know Dan and I and Juliet Weldon were going to do a sort of talk-in, brains trust, call it what you like, on the way writers work and so on, in the town here tomorrow evening, don't you?'

'No, I didn't know that,' Peter said. 'It sounds wildly exciting.'

'Don't sneer,' she said. 'These things can be quite exciting and creative if you approach them in the right spirit. A lot of people quite sincerely want to know all about people like us. Didn't Max tell you about it?'

'No.'

'Isn't that just like him?' she said. 'He takes no interest whatever in what I do. Well, it's a meeting of the local Arts League, who are really a very active crowd and they're holding the meeting at the Manor House Hotel, which is quite near us here at Grey Gables. It's got a very good big room for meetings. And the three of us, Dan, Juliet and I, were going to speak. I don't mean speak exactly. We were just going to sit there and have questions fired at us. They're expecting quite a big turn out, about fifty people or thereabouts, because of course Dan's a well-known figure here, apart from being rather famous generally. All sorts of people know about him since they did that television interview with him. But of all bloody bits of bad luck, he's gone down with gastric 'flu or something. He's really quite ill and there isn't a hope he'll be able to function tomorrow. So I thought—it just occurred to me as a possibility—that you might be persuaded to come down and take his place.'

'For God's sake,' Peter exclaimed, 'a

nice fool I'd look trying to be a stand-in for someone like Dan Braile!'

With her usual frankness, Kate replied, 'You were the only person I could think of, and I knew you wouldn't be offended at being asked at such short notice.'

'Oh, I'm not offended, I'm flattered at being asked to take the great man's place,' Peter answered. 'But I'm sorry, it won't do, Kate. Nobody's ever heard of me. Your audience would have a right to be disgusted.'

'But Peter, we've got to get hold of a man, we simply must, don't you see?' Kate said. 'Juliet and I alone just couldn't cope. We've got to have a mixture of the sexes. And if you came, the way we could set it up would be that we were three different sorts of writer, me a novelist, Juliet a short-story writer and you non-fiction, and we could compare the ways we work and really make it quite interesting, even if we're none of us up to Dan's standard. Of course the League would pay your expenses, your travel and hotel—I believe the Manor House is quite a nice place to stay—and the Committee have invited us to dinner beforehand and they might even pay you a fee. Not much, but something. So do come, Peter. It would be such a help. For one thing, it would stop Dan fretting. He's feeling terrible at letting these people down. He's like that, you know, tremendously conscientious. So it's making him worse.'

'But if it's simply a man you want on your panel—any man—' Peter said, 'why not get Weldon? He's staying down there with the Brailes, isn't he? He generally is when I hear of him.'

Walter Weldon, the husband of Juliet Weldon, was a critic who believed that he, almost alone, had created the recent Daniel Braile cult by the articles that he had written a few years before about Braile's earliest, otherwise almost unnoticed novels.

'Weldon—you don't mean it!' Kate said explosively. 'He's a disaster on a platform. First he gets so nervous that he can't bring out a word, then, once he gets started, you can't stop him. Besides, you know how he hates me. It's jealousy, of course, because

17

he can't stand Dan liking anyone but him, but he'd never miss a chance to get in some nasty digs at my books, which isn't the kind of thing we want at all. I mean, not at this affair. Of course he's got a right to his opinion of me and to state it freely in the proper place, but not on an occasion like this. We all ought to be frantically nice to one another to show the audience what delightful people writers are. So please come, Peter. Don't let me down.'

'I'm sorry, Kate, it isn't my kind of thing at all,' Peter answered stubbornly. 'If you don't want Weldon I'm sure you and Juliet will manage splendidly on your own. And perhaps Dan will be better tomorrow. These virus things, if that's what the trouble is, sometimes clear up quite suddenly.'

'He's been getting steadily worse for the last few days,' Kate said. 'And the silly man won't have a doctor. He's hopelessly prejudiced about drugs and things. Really, Peter, won't you come? Listen, I'll give you a little time to think it over and ring you again later.'

'It won't make any difference, Kate,' he said. 'I hate to say no to you, but apart from anything, I've my living to earn. I'm working pretty hard at the moment and I don't want to lose a couple of days, which is what this would mean.'

'Just think it over. At least do that,' she pleaded.

'It won't make any difference,' he repeated. 'Try to think of someone else for the job.'

'I'll ring up again later,' she stated, and rang off.

Peter laughed as he put the telephone down and returned to his chair.

'I suppose you gathered what that was all about,' he said. 'Kate really won't take no for an answer, will she?'

'I hardly ever summon up the energy to try saying it,' Max said, 'so she isn't used to it. But I didn't understand this thing about Dan being ill. What's the matter with him?'

'Apparently gastric 'flu.'

'Quite likely hysterical.' Max reached for the bottle of whisky on the table near him

19

and refilled their glasses. 'If you agreed to go down he might have a miraculous cure, just to make sure you didn't get any of his limelight. I'll tell you something, Peter, I'm getting a little tired of Dan Braile. I don't think he's good for Kate. I know she needs someone to hero-worship. She always has. There's always been someone around who's told her what she ought to believe about politics or poetry or diet or even clothes. But Braile's been interfering with her writing. He's been trying to get her to try for a depth she simply hasn't got in her and it's spoiling the kind of thing she can do well. Besides, there's something about that sort of community at Grey Gables that rather sickens me.' He drank some of his whisky. 'I'm just hoping it'll blow over some time soon. Her enthusiasms don't usually last long.'

'I didn't know you'd stayed at the place yourself,' Peter said.

'Yes, I did, for a week-end last autumn. I'd had 'flu myself and Kate said the change would do me good and took me down there.' Max gave a sardonic grin.

'What did me good was getting home again. They don't worry much about comfort. Actually I rather liked Braile's wife and that daughter of hers by her first marriage who was staying there too at the time. But there was a kind of hot-house emotionalism about the atmosphere that didn't agree with me at all. They made me feel I must be something abnormal in the way of a cold fish. And perhaps I am. Perhaps that's why Kate has to have these attacks of *Schwärmerei*. Now what was it we were talking about? Oh yes, criminals. Something about the attraction of getting to know one.'

But they had lost the thread of their discussion and began to talk of other things.

About an hour later Peter left for home. The telephone had not rung again, which had been a relief, for he was not by nature disobliging and did not enjoy refusing to do what he was asked. But Kate's request had appalled him even more than he had told her. He was quite at his worst on a platform. The old feeling of being all hands and feet always came back to him, while he could never control a tendency to slide backwards and forwards between flippancy and gravity in a way that his audience seemed never to understand. It was an experience that he usually avoided at all costs.

He had no car and went home by Underground. His telephone was ringing as he put his key in his door.

He cursed it. He was sleepy and mildly drunk and did not want another argument.

Climbing the stairs to his little flat very slowly, he hoped that the ringing would stop before he reached the top. But it continued inexorably and once he was in the same room with it he was not strong-minded enough to ignore it.

Picking up the telephone, he grunted, 'Yes?'

The voice that spoke was not Kate Rowley's. It was higher, much younger, much more appealing. He recognized it at once.

'Gina!'

Gina Marston was Daniel Braile's step-daughter. Peter had met her first a year before at a publisher's party to which she and her mother had been brought by Braile, then had met her a number of times afterwards and had thought of her more often still, though not in a way, he had convinced himself, that had disturbed his relationship with Caroline. Gina was simply a beautiful child with problems. A great many problems. And when one of them became too much for her she had a way of ringing Peter up and demanding advice, which he gave freely enough though he doubted if she ever followed it. Generally he never heard what became of her dilemmas. She was a curious mixture of openness and reticence, of trustfulness and wariness.

'Peter, Kate told me she rang you up a little while ago and that you refused to come here,' Gina said. 'But she told me she was going to ring you again when you'd had time to think it over. So I thought I'd talk to you first.'

'So you're staying at Grey Gables now,'

he said. Gina did not usually spend much time in her mother's home. She seemed to feel happier in the home of her father and his second wife. 'If I'd known that perhaps I shouldn't have refused to go.'

'I wish you meant that.'

'How's Dan?' he asked. 'Is he really ill?'

She did not answer his question. 'Why did you refuse to come?' she asked. 'Please, couldn't you do it?'

'Gina, as I told Kate, it isn't my sort of thing at all,' he answered. 'You know I never get up on platforms and speak.'

'But that isn't why I want you.'

'Isn't it? It's the reason Kate gave me.'

'Oh yes, that's why *she* wants you, now I've put the idea in her head.'

'You mean you suggested it to her?'

'Yes, I thought it was a wonderful way to get you to come down here without anyone wondering about it.'

'I'm afraid I don't understand you.'

He heard the telephone give an impatient little sigh.

'Peter, I need you,' she said. 'I've got

to have someone to advise me.'

'And I've got to get ahead with some work if I don't want to starve.'

'But surely you could spare a few days.'

'It's a few days now, is it? When Kate talked to me it was only one night.'

'Well, that would be better than nothing. But if you could stay a little longer, come to Grey Gables, talk to Dan... You see, there's something horribly wrong here, Peter.' She paused, then with a quiet deliberation which was far more effective than any tremulous appeal, she added, 'I'm pretty scared.'

It startled Peter for Gina was not a person given to dramatizing the problems that she brought to him. They seldom needed it. They mostly arose out of the difficult relationships between her two families and might easily have overwhelmed someone far more mature than a twenty-year-old girl.

His tone changed. 'What is it, Gina? What's really worrying you?'

'I can't talk about it on the telephone,' she said. 'Someone might hear. I may have been overheard already.'

'You haven't said anything very incriminating except that you want me to come down tomorrow.'

'Oh, won't you, Peter, please?'

'You're serious, are you? You really mean it about being scared? You don't have to elaborate now if anyone's listening. Just answer yes or no.'

'Then—yes.'

'When would you be able to tell me more about it if we're all going to be in a crowd at this panel affair?'

'If you came down a little beforehand I could meet you in the bar of the Manor House for a drink, say at six o'clock. The others will be coming along about six-thirty. Dinner's at seven and the show begins at eight.'

'If I come, you realize I'll be coming just for you and for no other reason. So if you're crying "Wolf!" heaven help you.'

'You know I don't do that sort of thing,' she said.

'Yes, I do know it, which is why I'm coming.'

'You *are* coming?'

'For better or worse, yes.'

'Oh, Peter, you're so good. I knew I could rely on you. I'll tell Kate and she'll book a room for you at the Manor House. I wish I could fit you in here at Grey Gables, but we're crowded out. There are the Weldons and an old woman called Alice Thorpe, who's a poet, and a couple called Paton—Cliff Paton's written some sort of novel—and me, of course, and—'

'Anyway, I'd far sooner be on my own,' Peter interrupted hastily, afraid that she might suddenly remember some small cranny in the big house into which he might be wedged. 'And I don't promise to stay more than one night.'

'Perhaps you'll change your mind when you get here. You see, there's no one, absolutely no one, I can talk to. And it's so awful, wondering—' She broke off. Her voice, when she went on, sounded quite different. Peter guessed that someone else had come into the room. 'So I'll meet you at six in the bar and brief you about the evening,' she said briskly. 'You'll find it's all perfectly easy. You'd better take a taxi from Sisslebridge, the buses are rather infrequent. And thank you so much for agreeing to help us out. Good night.'

She rang off.

Still holding his own telephone, Peter stood where he was, rubbing his long, bony chin.

The note of panic in the girl's voice had been too much to resist.

Yet if life at Grey Gables, as both she and Kate had described to him, had struck him as complicated, eccentric, neurotic, it was surely not in any way menacing.

So what had happened to put Gina into that state?

CHAPTER II

Peter found it easier than he had expected to explain to Caroline on the telephone next morning that he would have to cancel the arrangements that they had made to meet that evening.

He did not tell her the real reason. He told her only of Kate's appeal for help and said nothing of Gina's. He did not know why he did this. He was not afraid of Caroline's jealousy, for she seemed to be without it, a characteristic of hers that he had sometimes found annoying. Today she listened to him without asking him any questions, let a moment pass before she answered, then said it was a pity but that, as a matter of fact, she had been invited to a party that evening and had been thinking of cancelling their arrangements herself.

As he put the telephone down Peter felt a stab of uneasiness. He and Caroline had been doing a good deal of cancelling lately and with so little resentment on either side that it looked as if neither felt nearly as urgent a need for the other as they had only a little while ago. Was that the real reason why he had had the feeling recently that they ought to get married? A kind of insurance against losing each other completely.

A very bad reason, if it were so. But this drifting apart was happening so damned peaceably that it did not seem right to him. A few noisy scenes might have done them both good, he thought. Only it was very difficult to have scenes with Caroline. She avoided them gracefully but implacably and always forgave him with a touch of amusement for any of his attempts to pick a quarrel with her. It was almost as if she regarded him and his occasional explosiveness as a faintly ridiculous weakness of hers which she must remember never to take too seriously.

Yet she had seen something in him to love deeply for a time, he was sure of that, as he had in her, and their present casualness with one another sometimes gave life a distant bleakness. For a moment he almost telephoned her again to tell her that he had changed his mind about going to Sisslebridge and to ask her to change hers about going to her party. But he had given his promise to Gina and on the whole he was scrupulous about keeping promises. When he picked up the telephone presently it was to ring Enquiries at Paddington to find out the times of the trains to Sisslebridge.

It was raining when he reached it, which made the dusk of the early evening even darker than usual. Sisslebridge had a very dreary, windswept railway station. Puddles glinted on the unsheltered platforms as if the rain had been falling for some time, though it had been dry in London. It was heavy rain, and he was hatless and had no umbrella and his thick, sandy hair was soon plastered clammily to his head. It irritated him and made him feel ready to start complaining to anyone who gave him the chance. For instance, he would have liked to say to someone, why hadn't

Gina or one of the people at Grey Gables offered to meet him by car? He was going to a lot of trouble to oblige them, so why hadn't they put themselves out a little for him? It was all very well to tell him to take a taxi, but did such things actually exist in Sisslebridge? It seemed unlikely.

Nursing this thought resentfully, it was almost annoying to find, when he reached the station yard, that there was a long row of taxis waiting.

When he told the driver that he wanted to go to the Manor House Hotel and said he supposed he knew it, the driver answered, 'Oh, I know it. But d'you know how far it is? You might do better going by bus. Not that the bus goes to the hotel. You'd have a bit of a step the other end. It isn't that I mind going, you understand, it's just so's you know what you're in for.'

'That's all right,' Peter answered, pleased to remember that his expenses were being paid. 'I don't fancy even a bit of a step on an evening like this.'

'That's right,' the driver said as they

started. 'Worst spring we've had for some time. Been raining ever since dinner-time. Keep it up, the road to the Manor will be awash by morning. Always a bad bit of road, that. It's the hill. Rain comes down it like a river. You know the Manor?'

'No, I've never been there before,' Peter answered.

'Know Sisslebridge?'

'No.'

'Ah well, there are worse places, though it's changed a lot in the time I've known it. Used to be real country. Now we've got factories and all. Brought money to the place but I kind of liked the old ways.'

Sisslebridge, so far as Peter could see through the rain-spattered window of the taxi, consisted of a warren of council houses, one street of shops, mainly chain-stores and supermarkets, and a few old cottages with beams and thatched roofs, most of which appeared to have become antique shops. The shop windows all along the street were lit and sent shafts of light across the wet pavements, giving them a slimy glitter.

From the main street the taxi turned into an area of bungalows and after that went through some sort of industrial development from which lights shone out from factory windows, then it emerged briefly into the country, cruising bumpily along a bad road between high hedges. Whenever another vehicle passed, a wash of water sloshed over the windscreen of the taxi. The driver cursed wearily and said that he was glad he was not on the late shift.

'Be getting home to my tea after this,' he said.

Peter, glancing at his watch, wondered gloomily if there was any hope of tea at the Manor House Hotel at this hour, since it was still too early for the bar to have opened.

The hotel turned out to be a sizeable building of that stern red brick that never weathers, and had a hairy coating of Virginia creeper, not yet in leaf. A longish drive led up to the house from open gates. Its doors, in a porch decorated with concrete gargoyles, stood open.

Peter paid the driver, gripped his suitcase and went in.

He found himself in a passage which led up to closed glass doors. Beyond the doors was darkness. On his left a wide staircase with elaborately carved banisters led up also into darkness. Both passage and staircase were carpeted in aged, sickly pink. The wallpaper had probably once been pink too but had faded to a patchy mushroom colour, which a single light, hanging from a dusty, heavily moulded ceiling, made look indescribably dingy.

Peter looked round for an office labelled 'Reception' or 'Enquiries', where there would be a bell that he could strike to summon attention.

There was no such office, no bell. He stood there at a loss.

Then he heard somebody whistling. A door along the passage was kicked open and a youth emerged, carrying a tray. There was a collection of cutlery on the tray, so apparently the boy was on his way to lay some tables. It did not seem to occur to him that Peter was any concern of his and he would have passed him if Peter had not stood in his way.

'Good evening,' Peter said. 'My name is Harkness. I believe a room's been booked for me.'

'Oh?' the boy said.

He looked about seventeen, was spotty, with fair hair that curled over the collar of his rather stained white jacket, and he had small, vacant eyes that examined Peter as if he were an unfamiliar and possibly dangerous species.

'*Hasn't* a room been booked for me?' Peter asked, full of foreboding.

'A room, Harkness, yes, that's right,' the boy said, still with the air of its being nothing to do with him.

'Then can someone take me up to it? Perhaps it would be a good idea to get hold of whoever's in charge of Reception.'

'We don't have anything like that here,' the boy said.

'Then perhaps you could take me to my room.'

'What, now?'

'Yes, please.'

The boy did not move.

'I believe dinner's been booked too,' Peter said. 'At seven o'clock.'

'Dinner?' the boy said incredulously. 'Here?'

'For several people.'

'Oh. Ah. Yes, *that* dinner. That's right. You said you want to see your room.'

'If you'd sooner give me the key and some rough directions, perhaps I could find it by myself,' Peter suggested. 'And then I'd like a drink.'

'What, now?'

'Yes, please.'

'The lady hasn't come yet.'

'What lady?'

'Lady as looks after the bar. She'll be along any time now.'

'That at least is good news.'

'You want to see your room, then you'd like a drink,' the boy said carefully, as if he were trying to memorize a particularly difficult proposition. Putting the tray down on a table against the wall, he added, 'Come along up, then.'

He led the way up the wide staircase,

switching on dim lights as he went.

The staircase did not stay wide for long. As soon as it had turned the first corner and was out of sight of the entrance hall, it narrowed and one floor up became narrower still. The carpet was still pink, but looked even dustier than below and half the stair-rods had come adrift, so that it bulged treacherously from step to step, making ascent a matter demanding caution.

On a small landing the boy paused. In a half-whisper that seemed to Peter to have sinister undertones, he murmured, 'The bathroom's down *there.'*

He pointed down some steps, covered in sagging carpet, that led downwards into darkness.

'And your room's here,' he said.

He flung a door open.

A strong smell of mildew surged out at them. The dim, economical lighting of the room showed the source of it, a large, grey, furry patch of mould in the middle of the ceiling. The atmosphere was damp and cold.

Yet there was central heating in the room, a long radiator under the window. As the boy withdrew Peter crossed to the radiator and felt it. It was quite cold. Studying its ancient construction for a little, he turned some knobs, not very hopeful that this would make any difference to the chill of the room, then he unpacked his suitcase, combed his wet hair and ventured down the stairs to the bathroom.

It had once been a quite smart little place, black and white, with shining taps. But now, although the window was closed, rain was somehow coming in through cracks in the frame and a bucket had been put under the window to catch the drips. Only a few of them, however, actually fell in the bucket. Most of them were adding to a puddle on the floor, which it had occurred to someone to mop up by spreading a quantity of newspaper on the linoleum. The sodden newspaper, the sound of dripping, the cold and the memory of the smell of mildew in his room made Peter feel that if the lady who looked after the bar had not arrived by the time that he got downstairs, he would telephone for a taxi to pick him up immediately and go straight home again.

He found no one about when he went downstairs. The boy and his tray of cutlery had disappeared and silence had the whole place in its grip, which Peter was beginning to find eerie. Then, just as his temper had begun to rise, he heard a swish in the drive outside the wide-open door and, turning, saw that someone had just arrived on a bicycle.

A transparent plastic hood on the head of the newcomer suggested that it was a woman, though the long, heavy waterproof and rubber boots could as easily have covered the body of a man. She wheeled the bicycle into the porch and propped it against the wall, then advanced along the passage, untying the plastic hood and giving it a good shake, which scattered a spray of raindrops round her. Then, dragging a handkerchief out of a pocket, she mopped her face.

It was an old face with parched, yellow

skin drawn tight over sharp bones in a network of fine wrinkles. Yet her hair was thick and black, with just enough white in it to show that the colour was natural. She had big, black, brilliant eyes. Short and probably thin, though her bulky waterproof made it hard to guess at her shape, there was something odd about the way she stood, one shoulder high and her head a little on one side, in an attitude that gave her a look almost of coyness as she stood regarding Peter.

'Yes, you want something?' she asked, as if a person who wanted something were an unusual phenomenon in the Manor House Hotel.

'A drink,' he answered.

'A drink, yes. You wait a minute, I get it for you.' She was obviously foreign, though her accent was fairly good. 'You come this way, please.'

She led him to the glass doors at the end of the passage, pushed them open and turned on a light. Then she crossed the small room inside to an electric fire and switched it on.

41

'You sit here,' she said, indicating a chair beside the fire. 'Soon it gets warm now. Then I bring you a drink. But first I take off my coat and boots. What do you want, whisky?'

'Yes, please,' Peter answered.

'Yes, I think whisky for a night like this. Pity so much rain with so many people coming, but they come in cars so it makes no difference to them. On my bicycle I get wet. Now I go, but I come back.'

She disappeared through the glass doors.

The bar was really a quite pleasant little place, very different from what Peter had seen of the rest of the hotel. It had a big fireplace, intended for logs, but in which the electric fire made a comfortable glow. The walls were a soft green, there was a new green carpet and there were comfortable chairs grouped around low tables. Behind the grille that had been lowered over the counter a fine variety of bottles gleamed in shining rows.

A second doorway opened into a big, brightly lit room in which the spotty boy was arranging chairs in rows. The scene of tonight's meeting, Peter supposed, and wondered what the dinner would be like to which the Committee of the Sisslebridge Arts League was going to entertain him. He was feeling a little more optimistic about it than he had a few minutes earlier.

The small woman soon returned, rolled up the grille and poured out his whisky for him. She looked so pinched and cold that he was moved to invite her to have a drink with him. After a slight hesitation she accepted. Without her waterproof she appeared indeed thin, with bony wrists protruding from the sleeves of a much-washed, shrunken, purple pullover, and the reason why she had stood so oddly, with the inappropriate look of little-girl coyness, was also apparent. She was slightly hunchbacked. One shoulder was noticeably higher than the other and her head continually leant towards it. But her old face had a brightness that gave it surprising appeal. It occurred to Peter that she must have been beautiful when she was young, in spite of that malformed shoulder.

'You come to speak here this evening, isn't it?' she said, leaning on the bar, sipping her whisky. 'Instead of Mr Braile, who is ill. You know Mr Braile?'

'Only slightly,' Peter said. 'I've met him a number of times, generally at parties, where one doesn't usually get very far with anyone. Of course, I know his books.'

'Ah, his books, his books!' she exclaimed and clasped her hands. 'I have read them every one.'

'You admire him very much then?'

'Yes, yes. They are not easy for me, you understand, because the language is difficult, but I read them slowly from beginning to end, every one of them.' Her gaze grew worried. 'Do you not admire them also?'

'I've never quite made up my mind,' Peter answered, 'I always felt at the beginning that it's so good it could lead on to almost anything, and then when it gets near the end it seems to fizzle out and you're left wondering if it was ever really about anything.'

'Ah, you do not understand, you do

not understand,' she said. 'You must read them again, then the meaning will come to you.'

'I expect you're right,' Peter said. He was not arrogant about his literary opinions.

'Have you ever been to Grey Gables?' she asked.

Peter glanced at his watch. It was five past six already. Gina was late.

'No,' he answered.

'It is only a few minutes from here,' the little woman said. 'Their gate is almost opposite the end of our drive. They are very interesting people who stay there. And Mr Braile is not only interesting but a man of great heart. Yes, he is all heart, so wise, so kind. Sometimes he comes in here alone and we talk. Knowing him is one of the best things that has ever happened to me in this country. I am not English, you know. I am British subject for thirty years, but I can never be English. I do not mind. I come from Vienna and although I have forgotten nearly everything about it except the terrible day we fled from it, that is what I am, I am Viennese. Only

Mr Braile makes me forget that there are such divisions between people. It is a very good feeling. It is a pity he is not well. You should meet him here in his home and get to know him better.'

'I wish I could,' Peter said, not meaning it, because on the few occasions when they had met he had never been drawn to Daniel Braile as a man. Peter took more pleasure in his books than in their slight personal acquaintance. 'Ah—' He stood up. Gina had just pushed her way in at the glass doors. 'You're late, but it's so good to see a familiar face in this spooky place that I forgive you. What will you have to drink?'

She came to him quickly and kissed him.

It was obvious that she had walked through the rain. She had shed her waterproof in the passage, but the bottoms of her black trouser suit were wet and her shoes were muddy. She was a small girl, very slender about the waist and narrow about the hips, with long, fair hair, long, slender hands and almost childishly rounded features. Her eyes were curious. There was a noticeably dark rim round the unusually light grey of the iris which for some reason made them seem strangely intent and serious, and which always had such a hold on Peter's attention that when he looked at her he might have been trying to discover if there were some trick to it. She always looked straight back at him so that when they were talking they seemed to be inescapably locked to one another.

She said that she would like a gin and tonic, then went on in her light, soft voice, 'I'm sorry I'm late, Peter. It's so dark outside I took longer than usual to get here. I wanted time for a good long talk with you. Now I suppose we'll have to hurry.' She turned to the woman behind the bar. 'Hallo, Anna, you'll have a busy night for once, won't you, unless the weather keeps people away?'

'Ach, why should it matter to them in their cars?' the hunchbacked woman said as she poured out Gina's drink. 'Only I'm sorry your father is not well. Many people will be disappointed.'

'He's not my father, he's my stepfather,' Gina said with sudden fierceness. 'And we've got Mr Harkness instead, which I think is much more interesting. It's wonderful of him to come, because he simply hates this kind of thing. We ought to be very grateful.'

'Of course, yes, we are all very grateful,' Anna said, giving Peter a smile of apology. 'I do not mean anything. And I forget Mr Braile is not your father.'

She brought Gina her drink, then disappeared through a door at the back of the bar.

Peter and Gina sat down, facing one another.

'What is it, Gina?' Peter asked. 'What's the trouble? You can talk about it now, whatever it is.'

She gave a quick shiver and as if she suddenly wanted to postpone saying what was on her mind, glanced round in a puzzled way and said, 'What did you mean about this place being spooky? I've always thought it quite bright and cheerful.'

'Then you haven't been upstairs. It looks

as if no one's thought of disturbing the cobwebs for ten years.'

'Does it really? How awful. I'm sorry. I thought it was quite a nice place. I believe it was bought up by someone new a little while ago and he built on this bar and that big room where we're going to have the meeting. Perhaps he hasn't had time to get around to the rest. I'm sorry too that no one met you at the station. I've no car myself and I wanted a chance for us to talk before anyone else got hold of you.'

'It doesn't matter. Now go on and tell me what's wrong.'

She fingered her glass, then raised it quickly to her lips and swallowed some of the gin.

'It's Dan, of course,' she said. 'This illness of his. It sounds fantastic, but he's got it into his head he's being poisoned.'

'And is he?'

'Oh, Peter, please don't talk like that. This is serious.'

'Of course it is, but hadn't you better go on and tell me some more?'

She met his gaze with her straight,

deep look, which, as he had often found before, revealed very little of what she was thinking.

'It's his attitude,' she said. 'And everyone else's attitude too. There he is, horribly ill, and he won't have a doctor. He says if he had a doctor the poisoner would be found out and arrested and because the poisoner is someone he loves, he doesn't want that. He doesn't want revenge, he says. And all the time it obviously isn't poisoning at all, it's an ulcer or cancer or something like that and he knows it and he's just scared stiff of having to face it. And though I've never been fond of him, I don't like to think of him dying just because he's too frightened to go into hospital and have an operation.'

'Kate said he had gastric 'flu,' Peter said. 'Are you sure you aren't exaggerating?'

'That's what I mean!' she exclaimed. 'About the attitude they've all taken up. Kate and Mother and the Weldons and everybody. They all treat the trouble as if it weren't important. If Dan doesn't want a doctor, they say, there's no need to call one unless he gets worse. But I can see he's horribly ill already. I know it.'

'What are the symptoms?' Peter asked. 'And how long has it been going on?'

'It began about a month ago,' she said. 'He started vomiting and had awful pains and had to be carried to bed. It was supposed to be food poisoning. Then he got better and was quite all right for a few days, then it happened all over again. Then about a fortnight ago he had a worse attack than ever and he hasn't been out of bed since. He says he gets cramps in his legs and can't walk, but Kate says that's only because he won't get up and take some exercise. And he won't touch any food to speak of and his weight's gone down to nothing. And he looks...' She paused, wrinkling her forehead, searching for words. 'I don't know how to say it, Peter, because I've never seen anyone die, but I believe that's what I'm seeing now. Death coming. And all because he's too frightened to do anything about it.'

'And even your mother doesn't insist on a doctor?'

'Oh, she said she thought we ought to call Dr Barrow, but when Dan forbade it she just did nothing. She's never been able to stand up to him. You'll be meeting Dr Barrow presently. He's Chairman of the Arts League and much better at that than he is at medicine. Still, he'd be better than no one.'

'And what do you think I can do about it?' Peter asked.

She swallowed a little more of her drink.

'I thought—you see, this idea he has that he's being poisoned, perhaps he honestly believes it in a way. Perhaps he's convinced himself by now that it's true. Yet he's never really accused anyone special. He says it's someone he loves, which sounds as if he's pointing at Mother, but then he always says he loves us all, so that doesn't mean much.'

'Has he said all this publicly?'

'Yes, to all of us, and my feeling about it is that he's persuaded himself into such a distrust of the whole lot of us that nothing any of us can do will have any influence on him. But you haven't been near him all this time, so he can't have any suspicions of you. And so, I thought, if you would go and talk to him, he just might listen to you. I know it isn't a very good idea, but it's the only one I can think of.'

'But I hardly know him, Gina. I've only spoken to him a few times. He'll know you put me up to it.'

'But it couldn't do any harm, could it? And sometimes a sick person will take advice from a stranger when they won't pay any attention to their friends and family.'

'Yes, I think that's true.'

'So it just might work, you see.'

'If he agrees to see me at all.'

'Oh, he will. He likes you. He says he likes your unpretentiousness.'

Peter was not sure whether or not to take this as a compliment. There was more than a touch of patronage in it.

'Then what you want me to do is persuade him to see a doctor,' he said. 'That's all, is it?'

'Yes, what else is there to do?'

'I just wanted to be sure you didn't expect me to find out if there's any truth in this idea of his.'

He saw suddenly that she was trembling. But her voice was level. 'How could there be? They're all his friends. They practically worship him. I'm the only one who doesn't.'

'Yet apparently the only one who cares what happens to him.'

'I've never been dominated by him, that's all.'

Peter rubbed the side of his bony jaw.

'There's just one thing perhaps you haven't thought of,' he said. 'Suppose you're right and it's cancer. And suppose he knows it and has made up his mind not to fight it, but to let it kill him as quickly as possible. Wouldn't you say he's got a right to make that decision, if he wants to?'

'Oh, yes, I would,' she answered. 'I'm sure I'd never have the courage myself to go on fighting once I knew I'd something incurable. But if that's how it is, why all this talk about poison? Why deliberately make it harder for everyone else?'

'Perhaps his mind's wandering more than you've realized.'

She shook her head. 'It isn't. He's absolutely lucid.'

'That kind of thing can be awfully deceptive.'

He thought for a moment that she was going to burst into tears.

'Are you saying you won't help me?' she asked shakily.

'I'll be honest with you, Gina,' he said. 'I don't like the job at all. Talk of fools rushing in! But I'll see what I can do.'

She jumped up and kissed him again warmly on the cheek.

'Darling Peter, I do love you so! That's taken such a load off my conscience. It makes me feel I've at least tried to do something. Is that very egotistical, simply thinking of my own feelings? But you never know, it may work. You're a fairly overpowering person once you've really made up your mind to a thing!'

Just then a burst of sound from beyond the glass doors interrupted them. Footsteps and a chatter of voices approached the doors.

'Here are the others,' Gina said. 'We'll fix up the details later.'

CHAPTER III

It was not the party from Grey Gables.
The three people who came in, boisterously
laughing together, were all strangers to
Peter. Gina introduced them as Dr Barrow,
Chairman of the Sisslebridge Arts League,
Mrs Archer, the Secretary, and Miss Lyall,
the Treasurer.

Both the women wore long skirts and
glittering blouses. Dr Barrow was in a
tweed suit with a heavy black turtle-
necked sweater inside it. He was a tall,
thin man with sloping shoulders and a
hollow chest. The little that was left of
his hair was dark.

Anna had reappeared at the bar and he
bought drinks for the two women. Then
he clapped Peter on the shoulder.

'What a night to bring you down here,
eh?' he said in a resonant and pleasantly
good-humoured voice. 'Almost thought the

car would stick at the bottom of the hill. The road's inches under water. But we made it. Hope everyone else does too. Too bad if we don't get a good turn-out when you've taken the trouble to come all this way. Can't say how grateful we are to you.'

'I'm afraid I'm a poor substitute for Daniel Braile,' Peter said, as this certainly had to be said sooner or later.

'Not at all, not at all!' Mrs Archer said, then for some reason gave a shriek of laughter. During the evening Peter discovered that she laughed at nearly all her own remarks. She was about forty-five, plump and rounded, with thick, curly black hair brushed low over her forehead, heavily made-up black eyes and a purple mouth. 'Of course we can't all be Daniel Brailes, and we thought it a great honour that he'd agreed to come and talk to us this evening, but it's very good for us to see a new face. We do appreciate your coming. We're very inbred here, though we're very active. We have some splendid local talent. Miss Lyall plays the piano like an angel and Anna here has a beautiful voice.'

'Ach, me,' Anna said. 'Once. Not any more. My voice has gone.'

'It isn't true.' Mrs Archer gave another crow of laughter. 'And anyway, she has such an understanding of music, it's an inspiration for the rest of us. Then we have a drama group which I'm sure is far more adventurous and original than you'd expect in a place like Sisslebridge. Dr Barrow is its leading member, he's a wonderful comedian. And we have some quite distinguished painters living in the neighbourhood. We held an exhibition of their work here only last month.'

'And this lady is no mean performer on the harpsichord,' Dr Barrow said, winding an arm round Mrs Archer's waist. 'She gave a recital in this hall not long ago. We generally use it for our meetings. It's just about the right size for us and it has a very nice little stage at one end, as you'll see. Built on recently by Mr Danby, the proprietor. A very good idea. Sisslebridge has been needing something of the sort for a long time.'

Miss Lyall, a gaunt woman of about the same age as Mrs Archer, had sat down beside Gina, applied herself seriously to her drink and lit a cigarette. She spoke in a reedy voice. 'I hope they've made you comfortable here, Mr Harkness.'

'Oh yes, thank you, very,' Peter answered, feeling that the truth might spoil the atmosphere and that there was nothing to be gained by telling it.

'Good, good,' she said. 'I met someone the other day, I can't remember who, who said it had gone down. It always used to be very well spoken of. But of course so many changes have been happening in Sisslebridge since Lingstead's built their factory here—the electronics people, you know—and the whole character of the place has altered. Some people say for the better, some for the worse. I take the unpopular view. Unpopular in a group like ours, that is. I think it's a great improvement. It's meant a lot of new jobs for a lot of people who needed them and new houses being built for them—'

'Linda, Linda!' Mrs Archer interrupted

her. 'Spare us one of your lectures!' She turned to Peter. 'Perhaps it's lucky Mr Braile isn't here because he and Linda always quarrel when they meet. He thinks we ought to be tearing a lot of ugliness down instead of building a lot of new ugliness up.'

'Then why doesn't he start with that bloody great mansion of his?' Miss Lyall demanded, dribbling smoke from her nostrils. 'Hideous place. Give me a nice row of comfortable council houses any day.'

'You know you don't believe that,' Mrs Archer said and laughed very heartily. 'When Lingstead's first threatened to build here you were Secretary of the Save Sisslebridge Society and you fought tooth and nail to prevent them getting permission to come. And anyway, you live in one of the most charming houses in Sisslebridge yourself—a Georgian gem, Mr Harkness. Talk of council houses!'

'Well, we didn't save Sisslebridge, so we may as well make the best of what we've got,' Miss Lyall said. 'Mr Harkness, I've been meaning to tell you, don't let them give you a bill in the morning. That's all been taken care of.'

'Peter may not be leaving in the morning,' Gina said. 'He may be staying for a day or two.'

'Ah well, that's for him to arrange for himself,' Miss Lyall said. 'But your travelling expenses are of course our affair, so just send a note of them to me when you know what they are. Gina will give you my address.'

The glass doors from the passage swung open once more and Kate Rowley walked in.

She saw Peter and flung her arms wide. He accepted the inevitable and walked into them and was warmly embraced. But he extracted himself as quickly as he could. He could not have said why it was, but he had always felt mildly repelled by Kate. There was something hard and rough about her, too powerful, too grasping. Yet, in his way, he liked her. She was a short, sturdy woman of about his own age with a square, sensible face, brown hair cut very short and curling thickly round her head, blunt, strong features and bright, intelligent blue eyes.

One of the things that Peter did not like about her was that she should look so sensible and intelligent when in his view she was neither. He thought her excitable and emotional and astonishingly vain, vain about her writing, which consisted mainly of sombre Victorian novels about huge families of people who hated one another, except when now and again they achieved an incestuous love, and vain about her understanding of other people and the effect that she had on them. She seemed to feel sure that she was an intensely attractive woman and that her attentions must always be welcome. This evening she was dressed in shimmering dark red, with garnets in her ears, and certainly looked very handsome. When she had let Peter go, she went the round of the room, embracing everyone in turn, then accepted a whisky and soda from Dr Barrow.

Behind Kate came Helen Braile and after her the Weldons.

Helen was a tall, very shy woman, a few years older than Kate. She had a willowy body, soft brown eyes and dark brown hair that was brushed carelessly back from her face and rolled into a knot on her neck. She was wearing a rather beautiful dress of heavy black silk in which she managed to look gauche and dowdy. She nearly always looked dowdy except when she wore her oldest shabbiest clothes, in which she somehow achieved distinction. Giving Peter a limp hand, she murmured how good of him it was to come, refused a drink and sat down by herself in a corner.

The Weldons were both in a hurry to obtain drinks. Peter sensed something stormy in Walter Weldon that evening. He had the air of someone who has been interrupted in the middle of an argument and is still seething with all the things that he has not yet had the chance to say. He was about fifty, a slender man, dressed in a dark-grey suit, a pale-grey shirt, a spotted blue and white striped tie, and wore rimless glasses over his very bright, yellow-brown eyes. His face, which was small and crumpled-looking, was exceptionally mobile and vivid. He was a man who could always hold your attention when he chose to do so.

It was not always that he did. He barely nodded to Peter and to the members of the Committe of the Arts League, then said harshly to his wife, as if it were something that he was not saying for the first time, 'All the same, we should *not* have done it.'

She gave a big sigh as if indeed she had heard this before and was tired of it.

Juliet Weldon was a pale, vague-looking young woman with fair hair cut in a page-boy bob, an oval face and a rather vacant expression, as if she were lost in a dream. She hardly ever appeared to be listening to what was said to her, yet without warning she would suddenly enter a conversation with some remark of disconcerting shrewdness. She had come in jeans and an aged anorak.

'I tell you,' Walter Weldon said to the room at large, 'we ought not to have come.

We ought not to have left him. Helen, you aren't performing in this thing this evening. It doesn't mean anything to you. Why don't you go back and stay with him?'

'What?' Helen Braile said, jumping slightly, as if it scared her to be suddenly addressed.

'I'm only repeating what I said before,' Walter Weldon said in a tone of desperate patience. 'We shouldn't all have come out together. He's not in a state to be left alone. I think you should have stayed with him, Helen. Or you, Gina. The rest of us have obligations here and it would have distressed Dan if we hadn't fulfilled them, but one of you might have stayed.'

'Why not you yourself then, Walter?' Kate Rowley asked. 'You aren't performing.'

'You know I promised Juliet I'd be here,' he answered. 'There are some wives who find the presence of a husband a support, even if you yourself get on very well without. But surely Helen or Gina could have stayed with Dan.'

'I wanted to have a little talk with Peter,'

Gina said, 'to explain things to him.'

'Wouldn't Dr Barrow have been perfectly capable of doing that?'

'Not the kind of things I wanted to explain.'

'And what does that mean?' Walter stared hard at Peter for a moment. 'Have you been telling him all about poor Dan's delusions? I wouldn't put it past you.'

'Anyway, we haven't left him alone,' Kate said impatiently. 'He's got Alice and the Patons with him. So do stop fussing, Walter. You'll spoil the evening for everybody.'

'Aren't the Patons coming over here after dinner for the show?' Walter said. 'Anyway, they're all strangers. If Dan has a bad turn Alice Thorpe won't have the faintest idea what to do.'

'She knows she's to get in touch with us here. And she's promised to stay up till we get back. There's nothing to worry about.' Kate turned to Peter. 'Alice Thorpe is a poet, one of Dan's more recent discoveries. And Cliff Paton had his first novel published a few months ago and

Dan thinks it's quite important. He and his wife have been staying with us for some days.'

Peter noticed that 'us', it's proprietorial sound, and it grated on him. He went across the room to stand beside Helen Braile.

'I'm sorry Dan's so ill,' he said. 'It must be very worrying for you.'

She gave her brief, shy smile.

'He's rather good at being ill, you know,' she said. Her voice was soft and light, very like Gina's. 'I expect Kate's right that it's mostly psychological. His last book didn't do at all well and anything like that always upsets him. Last time it happened to him he had the most awful rheumatism for weeks.'

'But this upset sounds rather violent, from what Gina's been telling me.'

'Oh, Gina—she really doesn't understand him. Her feelings about him are so mixed. That's my fault, I suppose. Of course I wish he'd see a doctor, as she says he ought to, but I'm not so very worried.'

Kate bore down on them.

'There's nothing wrong with Dan that a little will-power couldn't cure,' she said. 'Will-power, a sensible diet and some exercise. How can he possibly expect to get well if he only picks at his food and stays in bed all day?'

'He *is* being very difficult,' Helen admitted. 'But if he really doesn't want to see a doctor, I don't see how we can force him to.'

Peter wondered if Helen had ever in her life forced anyone to do anything. When it came to leaving her first husband, for instance, and settling down to live with Dan, had any of the initiative been hers or had she merely mutely done what the two men had decided?

'I agree there's no point in his seeing a doctor if he won't co-operate,' Kate said brusquely. 'A doctor can't do much for a patient who won't answer questions and throws any pills he's given down the drain. I believe the best treatment for Dan would be a little healthy indifference. I'm so glad I managed to persuade you to come out this evening, Helen. You need a change.

You're looking a ghost.'

Helen certainly did not look particularly well. But then, she never did. She had a lack of vitality that always gave her a look of fragility.

'Ladies and gentlemen,' Dr Barrow said, suddenly raising his voice, 'I think it's time we went in to dinner. We want it over, with perhaps time for another drink after it, before the crowd starts to arrive. I always think it's a mistake to tackle this kind of thing cold sober. So let's go and eat.'

He came to Helen, drew her to her feet, took her and Kate each by an arm and led the way into the dining-room.

It was a big room, built mostly of glass and uncurtained. Although it was dark outside, raindrops could be seen slithering down the broad windows. Chairs had been arranged in rows in the body of the room, with the tables that would normally have been there cleared away to its edges. A table set for nine was on the dais at one end. There was a gaudy carpet on the floor, some decorative effects had been attempted with pot plants, the lights were bright and everything was new and clean. It could hardly have been more unlike the upper regions of the hotel.

Peter found himself placed between Mrs Archer and Juliet Weldon. Juliet showed no inclination to talk to him or to anyone else. Her private dream, as usual, possessed her. But Mrs Archer was quite happy to monopolize him, giving him all the insight that she could into the cultural life of Sisslebridge. They were waited on by the spotty boy. The meal was uninspired but edible, consisting of shrimp cocktail, steak, ice-cream and medium-quality Burgundy. Peter found his glass being constantly replenished. As Dr Barrow had promised, no one was to be forced to face the audience that night cold sober.

Afterwards Peter could not remember just how much he drank. If he had drunk less, he sometimes wondered, would he have reacted differently later? Would he have thought faster and more clearly? Would he have noticed certain things that simply escaped him?

But it was never difficult to persuade

him to drink and the wine and the brandy that followed it before the audience started to arrive had such a pleasant effect on his nerves that he actually began to view the performance ahead with pleasure instead of the dread that was normal to him at such times. He even forgot the discomforts that waited for him in the cold cavern upstairs when it was over.

He found another brandy waiting for him at his place at the table at which he, Kate, Juliet, Dr Barrow and Mrs Archer presently sat down, facing the audience that had been trickling in for the last quarter of an hour. Most of the women were in long dresses, the men in anything from dark suits and discreet ties to jeans and anoraks. They turned out to be a friendly audience, some of its members going to the trouble of catching Peter's eye from time to time and giving him a warm, personal smile, as if they had actually heard of him, or even read one of his books.

The questions that they asked were all the usual ones. Did the three writers who were kindly enlightening them on how they lived and worked write with a pen or straight on to a typewriter? Peter had long ago discovered that this is the one question about literature to which everyone has a burning desire to know the answer. Then did these particular writers work to set hours or only when fired by inspiration? How did they think of their plots? How much did they draw on their imaginations only and how much take from reality? Did they plan their work in detail before they started, or just write down what happened to come into their heads?

Kate treated all the questions with gravity, giving little dissertations on each, trying sincerely to give accurate, informative answers. Juliet spent a lot of time looking at her nails or into the distance and seldom thought of answering a question unless she was actually pressed to do so by Dr Barrow. Her answers then were swift, pointed and often amusing, but with an undercurrent of contempt for her audience that could not be missed. As the evening passed the laughter at her little jokes grew more and more uneasy. Peter found himself in a state of euphoria. Instead of the evening being an ordeal, he enjoyed it. From time to time he heard his voice running on and on, and, trying to put a stop to it, thrust his brandy glass away from him, resolving to drink no more until the evening was over. But presently he would find that he had drawn his glass back to him and that he was talking again, usually more flippantly than he thought was appropriate. But his listeners seemed to enjoy the sort of nonsense he talked to them. At times he felt the glow of profundity in his own words and hoped that he would remember what he had said long enough to make a note of it later.

Afterwards, back in the bar, when someone had given a vote of thanks to the speakers and the audience had got into their coats and their cars and driven away through the ever-falling rain, he asked Gina, 'Did I sound to obviously boozed up?'

She laughed. 'You know you never do.'

'I didn't disgrace you?'

'Darling, I've never known anyone who can sink as much as you can without showing a trace of it.'

'Your Arts League is admirably hospitable.'

They had been joined in the bar by the Patons, the young couple who were staying at Grey Gables. Cliff Paton looked about twenty-five and was tall and burly, with a thatch of fair hair that dwindled down along his jaw-line to a wispy beard. He blushed with embarrassed pleasure when Peter admitted that he remembered having read some good reviews of the young man's first novel. His wife, Rosie, was tall and dark and boyish, with hair cropped much shorter than her husband's and an aggressive nose. Her attitude to Cliff was protective and full of pride. With time she might turn into a dragon, Peter thought, but for the present her absorption in the young man was rather touching.

Anna, pouring out drinks, warned everybody that she would have to close the bar in a few minutes. Dr Barrow immediately ordered another round for everybody and

Peter found himself nursing yet another brandy.

'And you still want me to stay on and do this absurd thing?' he said to Gina.

'Oh, please.'

'Even when you know it won't do any good? Now be honest,' he said, 'you do know it won't do any good, don't you?'

She hesitated, her gaze, as usual, locking with his. He was in a mood to find her eyes not merely strange but extraordinarily beautiful. They were so grave, so intelligent, so honest, and at the same time, wasn't he right, so inviting? He had never seriously thought of making love to her before, but now he found himself wondering why he hadn't.

'I've told you why I thought it might, didn't I?' she said.

'That bit about his being ready perhaps to listen to a relative stranger.'

'Yes. Besides...'

'Well?'

'Oh, won't you do it just for me, Peter? You've heard what they're like. They simply don't take his state seriously.

And I—I'm very ignorant, you see. I suppose I'm what you might call rather young to try to take charge of things when there are so many older people around. Yet sometimes I feel as if I'm the only person there with a sense of responsibility.'

As if to contradict her, Walter Weldon suddenly sprang up from his stool at the bar.

'I can't stand this!' he exclaimed, his crumpled little face twitching with emotion. 'I'm going back. I know we should never have left him.'

'Oh, Walter, do sit down and keep quiet,' Juliet said. 'A few minutes can't make any difference. Finish your drink, then we'll all go back.'

'You needn't come with me,' he said. 'You can come in Kate's car. I'm going now.'

He darted out of the bar.

Juliet sighed deeply, as if she felt she had a great deal to put up with, and swirled the remains of her brandy round and round in her glass.

There was a longish silence.

Then Miss Lyall, the Treasurer, said to the room in general, 'I suppose we'd have heard some of Mr Braile's opinions about the changes in the neighbourhood if he'd spoken tonight.'

'Very probably,' Kate said. 'The lovely view from his terrace has been completely ruined.'

'And one man's view is more important than decent homes for a lot of people?' Miss Lyall said challengingly. She seemed to enjoy being at odds with most of the people there.

'It isn't one man's view.' Kate's gruff voice was abrasive. 'He always keeps the house as full as he can of people who need peace and quiet to find themselves in. He never had any himself when he was young. He lived in what was almost a slum in the Midlands and wrote his first book in a room where the radio was always on and his mother was working at her sewing-machine and there was a crashing and banging from the timber yard next door. So when he had the money to be able to do things for other people, what he thought of was peace. He wanted to be able to give them peace.'

'And to have a captive audience for his virtues,' Gina murmured in Peter's ear. 'There's no limit to the adulation he can swallow. But he *is* generous, you have to give him that. He'd even be generous to me if I let him and he knows I hate him.'

'Hate's a big word,' Peter said. 'Very few people who use it really mean it.'

'Is it a bigger word than love, then?'

'I don't know, perhaps it is.'

'You don't object to people saying they love each other, do you?'

'Not by any means.'

She laughed, drawing closer to him, so that her shoulder rested against his.

'But I think I do hate Dan, you know,' she said. 'Perhaps it's just a weak sort of hate, but it's there. He broke up my home, after all. I've got more or less used to it and since my father married again it's not been quite such a miserable place to live in as it used to be, but look at what Dan's turned my mother into. She's just a helpless sort of clinging creature, and I'm sure she used not to be like that.'

'Your view of her may have changed as you got older. And possibly she enjoys being helpless and clinging.'

'I don't see how anyone can.'

'Oh, they do. It can be a wearying business, standing on your own feet.'

'Now you're being sententious and it doesn't suit you. Of course I want to save Dan's life if he's in danger, although I still say I hate him. But I'm not a monster.'

'I suspect you might get quite fond of him, if you let yourself,' Peter said.

She gave a quick shake of her head. 'Oh no, not me. Haven't you ever hated anyone yourself?'

'I think so, when I was a child. And wanted to kill them, too, I rather think. But I was too frightened to do more than plot it. And luckily that intensity of feeling is something you grow out of. Hate's really a rather boring thing. It brings you so little in return.'

Somewhere a telephone was ringing. Anna went to answer it.

Peter looked at her. 'Are Anna and that spotty boy the whole staff of this hotel?' he asked. 'I haven't seen anybody else.'

Gina looked worried. 'And it's really awful upstairs, is it? There's something queer about it. I don't understand it. I wonder if it's anything to do with Lingstead's development. I mean, suppose Mr Danby bought the place, thinking he could make a really good country hotel of it, and he started improvements down here, then Lingstead's came along and he realized no one would ever want to spend their holidays in the middle of a factory area. Perhaps he just threw in his hand and let the place go.'

Anna reappeared.

'Mrs Weldon, the call is for you,' she said. 'Mr Weldon wants to speak to you.'

With an exclamation of surprise, Juliet got up and followed Anna into the room behind the bar.

There was a silence.

To Peter it seemed that there was a strange tension in the silence, as well as apprehensiveness on most of the faces in the room.

When Juliet came back there was apprehensiveness on hers and she was even paler than usual. He noticed that she spoke to Kate, not to Helen, which, in view of what she had to say, was curious.

'He's gone,' she said. 'Vanished. Walter was right, we ought not to have left him. He's got clean away.'

CHAPTER IV

Later Peter remembered what Juliet had said. He remembered the implication that Dan had not merely gone away but had escaped. But at the time, with the brandy that he had drunk beginning to make him drowsy, he took no notice of it.

They did not delay. Kate, Juliet, Helen, Gina and Peter left in Kate's car. The Patons said that they would walk.

When Kate realized that Peter was proposing to go with the rest of them to Grey Gables, she raised her eyebrows and said, 'There's no need for you to come, Peter. There's nothing you can do. I'd go to bed if I were you.'

Gina kept a tight hold of his arm.

'I want him to come,' she said.

Kate looked from one to the other.

'All right, get in,' she said.

It was raining more heavily than ever.

Crossing the beam of the car's headlights as it started down the drive, the drenching raindrops glittered like silver spears. But all around was the deepest darkness. The outlines of trees showed against the sky only like slight folds in the blackness. The hiss of the rain and its drumming on the top of the car filled the air.

At the bottom of the drive Kate swung her car to the left, drove only about twenty yards, then swung to the right through open gates and drove on along another drive between black banks of bushes. The shape of the house ahead showed up with surprising sharpness against the night because there was a light in almost every one of its windows. Peter could see the three pointed gables that had given the house its name. The porch light was on and Walter Weldon was standing at the door, waiting for them.

'I've been all over the house,' he said excitably. His features seemed to have shrunk into even tighter little crinkles than usual. 'I've looked everywhere. I swear to you he's gone. What's more, he got dressed. He's taken his waterproof and his beret and an umbrella and his gum-boots.'

'Thank God for that!' Kate said. 'I've been having a vision of him wandering about in this downpour in his pyjamas.'

'I haven't had time to check his suits,' Walter said. 'Perhaps he *is* in his pyjamas.'

They all followed Kate into the house.

'Helen, suppose you look into that,' Kate said. 'Go and see if there's a suit missing.'

Accepting the order as if it were natural for Kate to take charge here, Helen started up the stairs.

They were very like the stairs in the Manor House Hotel, with heavy, ornately carved banisters, but they were uncarpeted. Helen's footsteps made sharp clicking sounds on the bare boards as she went up. There was no carpet in the hall either. The floor was of black and white tiles, many of them cracked or chipped. The walls were painted white. A row of pegs in the porch held a number of coats, but there was no furniture. Except for the coats, the place might have been uninhabited. It spoke either of poverty or of deliberate austerity.

'And I found that damned Thorpe woman sound asleep,' Walter resumed with desperation in his voice. 'Would you believe it, she's left in charge of a very sick man and she settles down by the fire with her knitting and goes to sleep? I told you—'

'We know what you told us,' Kate interrupted, 'and I'll agree with you that for once you were right, but there's no point in going on and on repeating it. The question is—what do we do now? If he really isn't in the house. You're sure of that, are you?'

'Didn't I tell you I was?' A petulant snarl came into Walter's voice. There might be a serious quarrel between these two before long, Peter thought, if they did not discover Dan's whereabouts fairly soon. 'But go on, don't take my word for it, look for yourselves. Look in all the cupboards and under all the beds.'

'I think I'll do just that,' Kate replied.

'It'll be wisest in the end. And I suggest that someone comes with me to make sure I don't miss any suggestive clues. You, Gina, let's begin downstairs.'

She strode towards one of the doors that opened off the hall.

Just before she reached it, it opened and a very tall woman who was probably over eighty emerged. She wore a surprisingly short tweed skirt and several cardigans of different colours. Her very thin legs, in thick grey stockings, were knobbled with varicose veins. Her plentiful white hair was bundled on top of her head and more or less held in place by a very fine tortoiseshell comb. She wore what looked like valuable diamond ear-rings and a necklace of very artificial pearls. Her expression was gentle and diffident, although she had strong, almost fierce features. She was clutching a handful of tired-looking grey knitting.

'Oh dear, I'm so sorry, I seem to be dreadfully at fault,' she murmured in a soft, sweet voice. 'I left the door wide open on purpose so that I should hear him if he called me or rang his bell. Then I must have fallen asleep. I'm afraid I do that rather easily nowadays if there's nothing to distract me. Not for long at a time, you know. It's generally just a little nap. And presently I woke up and I thought, "That's odd, the door's shut." So I thought perhaps I'd only meant to leave it open and had forgotten to do it really. Or, I thought, perhaps the wind blew it shut. Only then it would have banged and I'm sure it would have wakened me. But of course I failed dreadfully in my duty to poor Dan and I simply don't know how to say how sorry I am.'

'It may have been Dan himself who closed the door,' Peter suggested.

Kate turned on him. 'Why should he do that?'

'So that Miss Thorpe shouldn't wake up while he was helping himself to boots and a coat and perhaps stop him or call you at the hotel.'

Kate considered it, then shook her head. 'He wasn't strong enough to do that without help—unless, of course, he's been faking recently, which I've half-suspected.'

'Well, let's get on with this search,' Gina said. 'Though why he shouldn't go away if he wants to, I don't understand.'

'At least it was inconsiderate of him not to let us know what he intended to do,' Kate said. 'He knew how we'd worry.'

She walked past Alice Thorpe into the room behind her.

After that Kate went quickly from room to room on the ground floor, followed by Gina. Peter and the Weldons remained in the hall. After a minute or two the clicking of heels on the bare boards of the staircase told them that Helen was returning. When she reappeared she was carrying a tray. On it there was a bowl of soup with fat congealed on its surface and a poached egg, obviously cold, on a piece of soggy toast.

'He didn't touch his supper,' she said. 'And his Aran sweater and his corduroy trousers are missing and so are his pyjamas and his razor and his toothbrush. So it doesn't look as if he just went out for a walk.'

'Really, Helen, who'd go out for a walk

in this weather?' Walter said impatiently. 'Why even suggest it?'

'It's just the kind of thing Dan might do, you know,' Juliet said. She had appeared to be taking no interest in what was happening, but suddenly, for a moment, gave the others her attention. 'At times he was mad enough for anything. And don't say he wasn't strong enough to go out. We all really agree with Kate, don't we, that he's been faking?'

'I do not,' Walter said. 'I most certainly do not. Of course I've realized that there was a psychological element in his illness and that he isn't as ill as he supposed, but even if his condition is partly mental, I'm assured he's a very sick man.'

'What about money?' Peter asked Helen. 'Has he taken any with him?'

She was standing in the middle of the hall with the tray in her hands, looking helpless.

'D'you know, I don't think he can have,' she said. 'He hasn't been to the bank himself or out shopping for several weeks, so I've been cashing our cheques and the money's all in my handbag. Oh, poor Dan—' Her voice caught as if she were going to cry. 'I can't help it, I feel something awful's happened. I don't believe he knew what he was doing when he got up and went out.'

There was a sound of footsteps on the gravel outside and the Patons came in, mopping their faces and shaking their waterproofs.

When they heard what had happened Cliff buttoned up his coat again and said, 'Rosie and I will take a look around in the garden. We're both wet already, so a little more won't hurt. Has anybody got a torch?'

'There's one somewhere in the kitchen,' Helen said, and drifted away with her tray through one of the doors opening out of the hall. She reappeared after a short time with a large electric torch. 'He's got one or two favourite places,' she said. 'You might try them. There's that summer-house at the bottom of the lawn where he's done a lot of his writing and there's the old barn behind the house where he does woodwork. I've been thinking he might have gone outside without realizing how hard it was raining and just taken shelter there.'

'With his pyjamas, razor and toothbrush?' Walter said.

'Why not?' Kate said harshly. 'Granted he didn't know what he was doing, he may have made his way automatically to one of those places and just stayed there, waiting to be rescued.'

'To the rescue, to the rescue!' Cliff Paton cried enthusiastically, as if this were a new, exciting kind of game. 'Come along, Rosie.'

Winding their arms round one another, the Patons tramped out again into the darkness.

Alice Thorpe had withdrawn into the room from which she had emerged and Peter and the Weldons followed her. Helen waited in the hall till Kate and Gina returned from their search of the house, then came into the room with them. A fire was burning in the elaborate Victorian fireplace and they all drew near to it. The fire was burning well but the room was cold. It was a big room with a high ceiling and three tall windows in a bay at one end. The walls were white, as they were in the hall, and the curtains at the windows a faded red. There were a number of easy chairs, all shabby, looking as if they had been picked up in a variety of sale-rooms, and a few nondescript rugs on the floor. There was one bookcase, overfilled with books, but there were no pictures or ornaments anywhere. The place made Peter feel uneasy. Austerity had never appealed to him. It chilled him more than the sheer cold of the room.

Sounding less certain of herself than usual, Kate said, 'What do you think, if the Patons don't find him, ought we to call the police?'

'For God's sake, Kate, don't lose your head,' Walter snapped at her. 'Dan hardly qualifies as a missing person yet.'

'I think he does,' she answered. 'I don't see how he can become any more missing than he is already.'

'And how pleased the police will be

if he strolls in in the middle of their investigation,' he said. 'After all, as Gina pointed out, there's no reason why he shouldn't go away and leave us if he wants to. He's got a perfect right to go wandering from here to London or anywhere else he chooses if he feels so inclined.'

'I still think we ought to call the police,' Kate said.

'What does Helen say?' Juliet asked. 'After all, he's her husband.'

Helen looked extremely flustered at someone having remembered that fact about Dan. She turned to Gina. It occurred to Peter that it was only very seldom that he was reminded of the relationship between the two. Gina paid occasional visits, like this one, to her mother, but neither showed many signs of affection for the other.

But Helen had to have someone to depend on.

'Gina, darling, what do you think?' she said.

Gina did what Peter had feared she might. She turned to him.

'Peter, what do you think?'

'I suppose I'd wait at least for a little,' he said.

'Of course,' Walter agreed with him. 'At least until tomorrow morning. Someone ought to stay up in case he comes wandering in in the middle of the night, and I'm quite ready to do that. And if he doesn't come back we can have another discussion about our best course of action by the light of day, when we'll all be more reasonable.'

'I consider I'm being entirely reasonable,' Kate said. 'I think we should lose no time in getting in touch with the police. However, if everyone's against me...'

She stooped, picked up the poker and gave the fire a sudden jab. Flames roared up the chimney. She crouched down, gazing deeply into it. Kate hated having to give in to anybody.

Helen gave a deep sigh and slid down into one of the chairs.

'I shan't sleep a wink,' she said. 'I feel as if—as if perhaps Dan's walked out of my life and I may never see him again. I

95

expect that's foolish, but it's how I feel. So I shan't sleep. So you go to bed, Walter. I'll stay down here.'

As if unconscious of what he was doing, he reached out and touched her hair in a gesture of the greatest gentleness. But as if the feel of her hair had burnt him, he jerked his hand away and gripped it with the other, as if to lessen the pain.

'I shan't sleep either,' he said. 'You go and get some rest, my dear. You need it more than the rest of us.'

'I would stay down here willingly,' Alice Thorpe said, 'as it's all my fault, but I don't suppose you'd trust me.'

Helen was looking up at Walter with an unfamiliar light on her face. He turned quickly away as if he did not want to see it and Juliet, staring straight before her, gave an abrupt little laugh, which sounded rather crazed, because it seemed to be at nothing.

Across the room Peter met Gina's gaze and found it trying to tell him something. He supposed that he knew what it was.

But it was no affair of his if Helen Braile and Walter Weldon were drawn to one another, or even were head over heels in love with one another. In fact, since he had been brought to Sisslebridge to talk to Dan Braile and Dan was not available, Peter saw no reason why he should remain at Grey Gables any longer.

Except, of course, that Gina wanted it. That was a powerful reason. More powerful than he had realized. A disturbing discovery. Or was it only the brandy working in him still, giving too bright a colouring to all his feelings?

The front-door bell rang.

It was the kind of bell that makes an extraordinary clangour. It seemed to echo off the bare walls of the room like an evil spirit, howling to get in.

Helen gasped. 'Oh God,' and clapped her hands over her ears, as if the sound terrified her.

Kate said, 'The Patons? No, they know the door isn't locked.'

Juliet said drily, 'The police, of course.'

Her husband turned on her. 'Why in

hell should it be the police?'

'Because, I suppose, they've found Dan somewhere, dead or alive, and have brought him home.'

Alice Thorpe gave a faint little titter of laughter. 'Oh dear, you're all like those people who turn an envelope over and over, trying to guess what's inside, instead of just opening it. I'm so sorry—of course I shouldn't laugh. I have a terrible habit of laughing at the wrong moment. But d'you know, you're all looking scared. Why doesn't one of you just go to open the door?'

'I'll go,' Peter said, and was crossing the hall when the bell pealed again in eerie summons.

He opened the heavy front door.

A young man stood there. He looked about twenty-five. He had wavy chestnut hair, elegantly styled and as strikingly handsome a face as Peter had seen for a long time. In fact, it was so perfect that it did not seem quite real. It felt to Peter a little as if a statue of a Greek god had been dumped on the doorstep and was addressing him with quiet, friendly good manners.

'I do apologize for arriving so late,' the young man said. 'The floods were the trouble. The Sissle has overflowed its banks. Terrible hold-ups again and again. I thought perhaps I ought not to trouble you at all at this time of night, but then I thought I'd just call in to say I've arrived in case Dan was worrying about what had happened to me. But I won't stay. I'll find a hotel somewhere and come back in the morning.'

He was wearing a dark-green corduroy suit and a pale-green frilled shirt with a chocolate-coloured velvet bow tie. Behind him in the drive Peter saw a pale-grey Jaguar, looking in the relentlessly falling rain like an island in the middle of a shiny lake.

'Dan was expecting you, was he?' Peter asked.

'Why, yes, I assume so,' the stranger answered. 'Hasn't he mentioned it? My name's Adrian Rolfe. If I'm not expected —I mean, if the dear man has simply forgotten about me—I'll just go away. I don't want to be any trouble to anybody.'

'No, no, come in,' Peter said. 'He probably mentioned it to one of the others. But we've all had rather a lot on our minds this evening, so I haven't heard anything about you myself. But I don't actually belong here. I'm sure Mrs Braile knows all about you. Come in and meet her.'

Peter did not feel at all sure that Helen knew anything whatever about Adrian Rolfe. If she did, she would surely have mentioned it. But it seemed important not to let the young man go. A stranger arriving so late on just that night might conceivably have something to tell them about Dan.

'Thank you,' the young man said, stepping into the hall. 'As a matter of fact, apart from the floods, I lost my way once or twice. I didn't realize how far you are from Sisslebridge. Dan's letter gave me the idea you were just on the edge of the town and his directions, I'm afraid, were confusing rather than helpful. Of course, that isn't surprising, is it? I've never thought of him as a practical kind of man, and he doesn't drive himself, does he? I believe I remember his telling me so. So he wouldn't know much about the roads.'

'You know him well, then?'

Peter was just about to shut the door when the Patons reappeared behind the newcomer. They came into the hall, still embraced, and stood dripping water on to the black and white tiles.

'Not a sign of him,' Cliff Paton said, disentangling himself from his wife and beginning to unbutton his waterproof. 'But it isn't easy to search on a night like this. We could easily have missed him if he'd fallen under a bush or something. Still, we looked as carefully as we could.'

'We really did,' Rosie said. 'We looked in the summerhouse and the barn and down the drive and amongst all those rhododendrons on each side of it and some way along the road too, in case he'd fallen into the ditch. We went as far as the bottom of the hill, where the water's quite deep.'

'Indeed it is,' Adrian Rolfe said. 'I

thought I was going to get stuck there, but I managed to come through it all right.'

'Of course he might have been able to wade through it,' Rosie went on, 'though I think it would have come over the tops of his gum-boots. But we didn't think he'd have managed it. So we thought of going back to the hotel and asking if anyone had seen him, and we caught Anna, just as she was leaving on her bicycle, and she was awfully upset when she heard what had happened, but she hadn't seen him.'

'So then we came back,' Cliff said.

'Excuse me,' Adrian Rolfe said, 'is this Dan you're talking about. Has something awful happened?'

'As a matter of fact, yes,' Peter said. 'Or probably. Dan seems to have vanished.' Then he remembered to introduce Rolfe and the Patons to one another. 'Now come in and meet Mrs Braile.'

He led the way to the sitting-room.

They were all just as he had left them, silent, and all had their eyes on the door. It felt wrong to Peter. It would have been normal, it seemed to him, for at least one of them to have followed him out to see who had arrived. The thought crossed his mind that they had remained as they were because they were keeping an eye on one another. But what had made him think of such a thing? What was happening to him? They were all worried, naturally, because Dan was ill and none of them knew for certain how gravely, and his disappearance suggested that he might be mildly deranged. So they were feeling guilty because they had not taken their responsibilities to him as seriously as they should have. That was all. There was nothing sinister in their evident helplessness and distress.

He introduced Adrian Rolfe to Helen, then to the others in the room.

Rolfe advanced and shook hands with Helen.

'Is it true that I'm not expected?' he said. 'Did Dan really forget to tell you that I was coming?'

His handsome face looked politely rather than deeply troubled. It was not a face intended for expressiveness. Serenity suited it.

'Well, I'm afraid...' Helen began, then gave up and did not try to finish her sentence.

Kate took over. 'We don't even know who you are.'

'Not that that's against you,' Juliet murmured. 'Though we don't care to admit it, there are so many people we don't know.'

'You're a friend of Dan's, I assume,' Walter said.

The lack of warmth in this welcome did not seem to disturb Adrian Rolfe.

'Well, yes and no,' he answered. 'In a sense, yes, we're most intimate friends. But actually we've never met.'

'Oh, one of those,' Kate said. 'A pen friend, is that it? You wrote to him, I suppose, to tell him all about some burden you had on your soul, and you got a charming letter back from him, and that gave you the idea he simply couldn't wait to meet you. Only you picked an unfortunate time for calling on him because it happens he's vanished away into the night without giving any of us a hint as to his whereabouts. Which suggests, at least, that he didn't feel it was important to stay around to meet you.'

'Kate, is there any need to be rude to Mr Rolfe?' Walter asked, automatically taking Rolfe's side because Kate had decided to be unpleasant to him. 'You haven't given him a chance to explain himself. I apologize, Mr Rolfe, if we're behaving rather oddly. But we're all very worried about Mr Braile. He's been seriously ill for some time, then this evening, when for once most of us went out together, he suddenly got up and disappeared.'

'Then I'm very sorry I intruded at such a time,' Rolfe said. 'And as it happens, Mrs Rowley's guess about my relationship with Dan is not so far from the truth, except that I didn't come here on the strength of one letter from him. We've been corresponding for over a year. I've a collection of wonderful letters from him. I wrote to him out of the blue—I had to, I couldn't control myself, though it isn't the kind of thing I'm in the habit of doing—and I had a letter back from him in which he invited me to write again. So naturally I did so and again I had an answer. And soon we got into the way of writing to one another every two or three weeks and after a little while he started inviting me repeatedly to stay at Grey Gables. At first I was too nervous to accept. I felt—does it sound absurd?—I felt actually scared of meeting him, in case the real, living man shouldn't be like the dear friend I'd got to know on paper. But at last we arranged that I should come here today, and I should have been here a couple of hours ago, as I was telling Mr Harkness, if it hadn't been for the flooding I ran into and for very stupidly losing my way. And now I think I should say goodbye to you all and leave you in peace, hoping most sincerely that your worries about poor Dan will prove exaggerated.'

'Oh, but you must have a drink before you go!' Gina suddenly exclaimed, darting forward. 'We can't send you away on a night like this without a drink to warm you up. And the Patons too—they're soaked. And all the rest of us, if it comes to that. Peter, come and help me get the things.'

She caught hold of his sleeve between a compelling finger and thumb and swept him towards the door.

He went without resistance, though without understanding what had moved her. When he had closed the sitting-room door behind them, he withdrew his arm from her grasp.

'What's got into you, Gina?' he asked. 'What are we supposed to be doing?'

He wondered if Rolfe's good looks could so have gone to her head that she had had this unexpected attack of hospitality.

'Getting drinks,' she said. 'Come along.'

'And what else besides drinks? I'd have thought we'd all had more than enough already.'

'Come along to the kitchen,' she said. 'It's just an idea I had while we were talking to that man. We've an opportunity to look at something. If we wait we may be too late.'

She hurried him along to the kitchen.

It was an old-fashioned kitchen in which next to nothing had been spent on modern conveniences, except for an electric cooking stove and the installation in the tiled alcove that had once probably held an old range, of a coke-burning boiler to provide hot water.

Gina, looking round, drew her breath in with a sharp little hiss of dismay.

'What's the matter?' Peter said.

'We're too late already.'

'Too late for what?'

'His tray,' she said. 'I thought...'

'Gina, what's all this about?' Peter demanded.

'It's gone,' she said. 'Well, it doesn't matter. Let's get the drinks and go back.'

He took her by the shoulders. Her eyes were tragic.

'What is it, Gina?'

She shook his hands off. 'Nothing. Really nothing.'

'Tell me,' he said.

'Well, you see,' she answered, 'I had the bright idea we might be able to find out if there's really been any poison in Dan's

108

food. I thought perhaps you could take samples of it away and get it tested. And if it was all quite wholesome we could be fairly sure his illness had nothing to do with poison. But someone's washed up the things that were on the tray. The soup's gone down the drain and the poached egg's probably in the boiler. So there's no evidence either way.'

'And of course you've realized,' Peter said, disliking her for the moment, 'that the only person who's been in here and could have done the washing up is your mother.'

CHAPTER V

She turned on him in a blaze of fury. He had an impression, which could only be imaginary, that the dark rim round the pale grey of her eyes had suddenly grown broader, giving them a metallic hardness.

'I wanted to clear her, can't you understand that?' she hissed at him. 'That's all I wanted. You talk as if I was looking for evidence against her.'

'But she's the only person who's been in here. She came in to fetch the torch for the Patons. And it seems she used that minute or two to destroy the evidence that might have told us something.'

'So you think she's been poisoning him!'

'I don't. I really don't, Gina.'

'I saw it in your face.'

'Only because you'd decided you were going to see it. Now what about those drinks we're supposed to be fetching?'

Without saying anything more and still with that air of dangerous anger about her, she took him to the dining-room, where they put bottles and glasses on a tray which Peter carried into the sitting-room.

They had all sat down. Adrian Rolfe was beside Kate on the sofa. She seemed to have abandoned her hostility to him and looked rather as if she would like to offer him one of her generously distributed embraces.

She was saying, 'Actually it's just like Dan not to have told us anything about you, Mr Rolfe. He's very secretive about all sorts of things. For instance, he'll never discuss his work with anyone or let anyone have a glimpse of it until it's quite finished. And he likes to go off to London alone—he's got a small flat there—and he never tells any of us a thing about what he does there. This was before he got ill, you understand. We all accepted it as a matter of course. A man like him must have a far greater need of privacy than the rest of us. And I can't help wondering if you're the reason why he vanished this evening. But don't misunderstand me. I don't mean it was your fault. I only mean that perhaps suddenly he felt he couldn't face meeting a stranger and had to get away. That would be just like him. Don't you think so, Walter?'

'I do not. I think you're talking nonsense, Kate.' Walter was pouring out the drinks. He put a glass into Rolfe's hand. 'However, it looks as if you may have had your drive down here for nothing, Mr Rolfe.'

'Oh, it won't have been for nothing,' the young man replied thoughtfully.

An ambiguous remark that brought a brief silence after it.

Then Kate said, 'At least it's a possible answer to the question of why Dan dragged himself out of bed and vanished into the night. And it makes me inclined to agree with you, Walter, that we ought to wait to inform the police until the morning. Dan would be very angry with us if we'd done that when he was simply hiding out somewhere.'

'That's settled then,' Walter said. 'I'll stay down here tonight and if he hasn't come back by the morning we'll go to the police.'

Adrian Rolfe drank his drink rapidly and stood up. Once more he apologized for having intruded at such a difficult time, asked if anyone could tell him of a hotel near at hand, and when Peter told him that the Manor House was only just across the road, though perhaps it was not to be too warmly recommended, replied that he was not at all fussy and that he was sure that it would suit him splendidly.

For Peter this had the advantage that he was given a lift back to the hotel in the Jaguar and did not have to plough his way back on foot through the rain.

They found the door of the hotel still standing open but no one about.

Waiting for a little while in the passage, they listened for a footfall or the sound of distant voices, but there was only silence.

'We can't actually be the only people here, can we?' Rolfe said. 'Can the place be run by invisible magic hands?'

'Well, I warned you,' Peter said. 'The staff is a little inadequate.'

'But doesn't one have to register?'

'I haven't been asked to do it myself.'

'And I was hoping for a meal of sorts. I'm extremely hungry.' Rolfe looked round, frowning. 'There must be a kitchen somewhere. Perhaps we could raid it.'

'Listen!' Peter said, holding up a finger. 'I heard—I think I heard—'

'Yes, yes,' Rolfe said. 'Music. A radio. If we can track it down we may find food and warmth and welcome.'

'That's going a bit far,' Peter said, 'but perhaps we can get you a sandwich.'

He set off in the direction from which the music was coming.

They found the spotty boy in a kind of pantry, crouched over a transistor with a look of dreamy enchantment on his face. It was only with great reluctance that he was persuaded to tear himself away from the source of what was possibly the only pleasure in his life and show Rolfe to a room. With even greater reluctance he agreed to provide sandwiches and coffee.

They took a long time to appear. Rolfe and Peter, who had also ordered coffee, waited for them in the bar. Rolfe's earlier loquacity seemed to have run out. He sat there silent, with a complete absence of expression on his handsome face.

After a while Peter said, 'If you don't mind a question, I suppose you can't tell us anything about Dan's disappearance?'

Rolfe raised his eyebrows. 'Is that a question?'

'What I meant,' Peter said, 'is did you by any chance have some arrangement with him to come here, collect him and take him away and then go back to the house to see what the people there were doing about it?'

'Not by any chance, no,' Rolfe answered.

'One of the problems about his disappearance, you see,' Peter went on, 'is that no one thinks he was well enough to go away without help.'

'Wasn't there anyone left behind in the house who might have helped him?'

'Only Miss Thorpe and I think she's over eighty. Tough, however. Perhaps she could have done it. And there were the Patons. They stayed behind while all the rest came over here for dinner, but they turned up soon afterwards for a sort of debate we had, run by the Sisslebridge Arts League. Dan was supposed to have spoken in it, but he was too ill, so I got hauled in. That's why I'm here.'

'Ah, I've been wondering about that,' Rolfe said. 'Perhaps I ought to tell you the real reason why I'm here myself. I haven't told you the exact truth about it.'

'I rather thought perhaps you hadn't.'

The spotty boy came in then with the sandwiches and coffee. The sandwiches looked lumpy but sustaining. Rolfe fell on them hungrily and finished one before he went on to explain himself further.

'Dan never invited me to come down,' he said. 'He seemed to have rather the same sort of feeling as I had that we were getting along splendidly on paper and that meeting might spoil it. But then a few days ago I got a very curious letter from him. A very disturbing letter. He'd told me by then that he wasn't well, but he'd rather made light of it. Talked of having picked up a bug and what a nuisance it was because he didn't feel up to working. Then I got this letter...' He bit into another sandwich.

'About poison,' Peter said.

'Oh, so you know about that.'

'It happens to be the real reason why I'm here too.'

'How's that?' Rolfe asked.

'Gina, Dan's stepdaughter, wanted me to come down to help convince him that, whatever was the matter with him, he ought to see a doctor.'

'I see. That's curious, in a way, in view of what he wrote to me. He wrote that he felt he had to tell someone what was happening and that I was the only person he could trust because we'd never met. That meant, apparently, that I couldn't be involved in the trouble here. And the trouble was that he was nearly sure he was being poisoned. But it wasn't the kind of thing, he said, that you can possibly be absolutely sure of unless you can make tests. He might be doing someone a great wrong. But he didn't want a doctor in case it turned out he was right and it led to police action, a trial and all sorts of things he dreaded. He said what he wanted was to get away but that he felt too weak for it at the moment. And then he said that if he couldn't get away and if I heard he was dead and there was a post-mortem and they found poison, I wasn't to interfere unless the wrong person got arrested, the right person being—you aren't going to like this—his stepdaughter, Gina.'

'Gina!' The anger that could still flare in Peter without any warning, the anger that had made him feared as a boy and that he had come to fear in himself, blazed up through his veins like sudden fire. He could feel the flames of it in his face. 'The slandering bastard! She's the only one there who cares enough about him to try to get him cured.'

Rolfe made a gesture of apology. 'I'm only telling you what he wrote. I told you you wouldn't like it. You're in love with her.'

'I am not!' Peter, in his fury, almost shouted at him. Then he wished that he had not answered at all. The man had no reason to expect it of him. 'Gina's a child,' he muttered, doing his best to jam the lid down tight on his rage. 'And a remarkably good, honest and generous-minded one. It's vile of Dan to make an accusation like that.'

Rolfe gave him a sardonic look. 'A quite mature sort of child, I thought,' he said. In a tone of detachment he added, 'Some poisoners have been very attractive young women.'

'Slandering bastard,' Peter muttered again, feeling that the repetition was calming. 'I've been worrying about him a lot this evening, but now I don't care if he's got drowned in the floods. There's something unreal about this whole business. I'm beginning not to believe in anything that's been happening. I shouldn't be surprised if the whole lot of them know where Dan's gone.'

'Including Gina?'

'Except Gina! The whole thing could be some sort of publicity stunt. In which case, of course, you and I have both been made use of as witnesses to how upset and surprised everyone was. Dan must have known the sort of letter he wrote to you would bring you down here, and it was Kate Rowley, not Gina, who originally asked me to come. When I wouldn't, she must have put Gina on to it. Gina isn't particularly subtle. She'd never notice if she was being manoeuvred.'

'Tell me a little about her,' Rolfe said. 'Has she anything against Dan?'

'She holds it against him that he broke up her home,' Peter said. 'She's very attached to her own father. But she stays at Grey Gables now and then so that she can be with her mother and she seems to have accepted Dan as a kind of addition to the family.'

'What sort of man is her father?'

'I've never met him. He's a professor of chemistry or something at London University. Helen was a student of his. She married very young and left him about seven years ago. I believe it was fairly amicably arranged. They still see each other occasionally. He married again about a year after the divorce and Gina seems to like her stepmother. She was an actress but gave it up when she got married.'

'What does the girl do herself?'

'She's a student.'

'Also of chemistry?'

'No, of modern languages—' Peter suddenly saw where the other's questions were leading. 'You're suggesting that if she had access to a lab she could easily have laid her hands on some poison.'

'The thought just crossed my mind,' Rolfe admitted.

'Listen,' Peter said, striving hard to keep hold of his unreliable temper, 'I've told you Gina's the one person in all that crowd who I'm absolutely certain has had nothing to do with whatever's been happening there.'

'Yes,' Rolfe said, giving a slow nod of his head, 'that *is* what you told me.'

'Doesn't her wanting to call in a doctor prove it?'

'If, when it comes to the point, she really tries to have a doctor called in. So far

Dan's been refusing to have one, so she's been safe in saying that he ought to.'

Patience, Peter said to himself, patience. He leant back in his chair.

'While we're on the subject,' he said, 'what do you do yourself? You blow in from nowhere, ask questions and admit you told some lies about why you came and seem to think there's no need to say anything more.'

'In the sense I think you mean it, I don't really do anything,' Rolfe said. 'I'm reasonably rich, having had an industrious father in the machine-tool trade, and I play at this and that with more or less seriousness, as the case may be. Dan Braile and his work happen to be one of the things I'm very serious about, so if I start playing detectives now you can take it I'm serious about that too. But don't mistake me for a professional. The thought that I might be was beginning to worry you, wasn't it?'

Peter had the feeling that the young man was altogether too perceptive to be comfortable company.

'To borrow a phrase from you,' he said, 'the thought just crossed my mind.'

'Then forget it. I'm very worried about Dan and I'm consumed with curiosity about him, but that's all. Now I'll be off to bed. I wonder if anyone in this strange den will oblige by giving us breakfast in the morning. Perhaps I'll see you then. Good night.'

'Good night.'

They both went up to their bedrooms.

As Peter opened the door of his a blast of hot air blew out at him. Apparently the twiddling of the knobs on the radiator that he had done on his arrival, without much hope that it would affect the chill of the room, had raised the temperature of the water in the old pipes almost to boiling point. They were clanking and making bubbling noises. Wondering if they might possibly explode if he left them as they were, he hurriedly turned the knobs in the reverse direction.

Strangely enough, the smell of mildew in the room seemed even stronger than before, as if the slight cooking that the

123

patch of mould on the ceiling had been undergoing had increased its pungency. He opened a window. But the rain splashed in on the window-sill, so he closed it again and, resigning himself to the peculiarities of the room, went to bed.

It was some time before he fell asleep. Perhaps because of the excessive heat of the room, he was restless and his brain stayed irritatingly active. He thought about Daniel Braile. What sort of man was he? Adding together all that Peter had heard about him that evening and all that he had thought about the man himself at different times, what sort of picture emerged?

Beginning with his books, what did they tell one about him?

It had to be admitted that in an age much attracted to ugliness, Dan found beauty in unexpected places, writing of it with an insight and sincerity that was all the more convincing because the language in which he did it had a complex and brilliantly coloured beauty of its own. In an age of violence, he chose to write of the mild and gentle. At a time when much ink and paper went to the bare mechanics of the sexual act, he wrote of affection and tenderness. People who decried him accused him of sentimentality. But they were wrong, Peter thought. Dan Braile could write of the hard things of life, envy, meanness, death and decay, with detachment and power. Yes, he was quite a writer, there was no getting away from it.

Yet Peter wanted to get away from it because he had never liked the man himself. But what he wrote must surely be the real Dan. More real than the rather touchy and aloof human being whom Peter had met a few times and who, in a fumbling sort of way, had seemed to want to be friendly, only to withdraw suddenly, as soon as Peter responded, as if it had just occurred to him that to be too friendly might be beneath his dignity.

Dan was a tall man with wide shoulders, a slight stoop and a rather graceful, prowling way of walking. He had hair that had once been dark but now was silver-grey, and dark eyes that could look luminously attentive or coldly bored. He had a long, narrow face, a thin beak of a nose and a small, soft, solemn mouth. That mouth was certainly one key to his personality. He had very little humour. He took himself and others with the greatest seriousness and Peter had never met anyone like him for making any flippancy fall flat with a dull, most humiliating thud. An intimidating man in his way, singularly skilled, even if he did not entirely mean it, at making you feel foolish.

But what about this illness of his and his disappearance?

Kate Rowley seemed to think that the illness was largely hysterical. Walter Weldon appeared to be acutely worried about it. Juliet Weldon seemed not to care much one way or the other. But Juliet cared very little for anything but herself and the strange, subtle, rather frightening little stories that she wrote. Gina believed that the illness might be cancer. What the Patons and Alice Thorpe, almost strangers in Dan's little community, thought about the matter did not seem important. Dan himself had been making general accusations that he was being poisoned and had actually written to a young man whom he had never met to tell him so and to accuse Gina of being the poisoner. Then, very sensibly, if there was anything in his suspicions, he had vanished, choosing an evening for it when there had been no one in the house but a drowsy old woman, so that he had been able to dress and escape without attracting attention.

He could have had it planned for some time. It had been just his bad luck that that evening had turned out to be the wettest that there had been for several months. However, if he had been capable of walking away through that rain, even with umbrella and gum-boots, then he could not possibly have been as ill as he had made out.

So had Peter been right that the whole thing had been aimed at achieving publicity?

He did not really believe it. He thought that Dan was too sincere a man, with too much sense of his own dignity to descend to such vulgarity. But plainly he was a very different person to different people and all of them might be at least partly right.

Anyway, he was no longer any concern of Peter's. Gina had wanted him here to persuade Dan to see a doctor and if Dan was not available there was no reason why Peter should not go home next day.

But dropping off to sleep at last, he was aware that he was not as anxious to go as he would have expected. At least, he thought, he must see Gina again before he left. His last waking thoughts were distractingly filled with her image.

Some time in the night the rain stopped. The morning was grey and cold and still. The heavy sky looked as if it might pour down torrents again at any moment. Peter went to a window and looked out. He found what he had not discovered when he had arrived in the dusk the evening before, that his room faced directly towards Grey Gables, the roof of which, broken by the points of the three gables, showed above some pines along the roadside.

In the hotel garden clumps of daffodils, battered by the rain, were lying flat in the grass. The bare branches of trees, not yet in leaf, glistened with moisture. The drive down to the gate was blotched with puddles.

Someone was coming up the drive on a bicycle. Anna. So the spotty boy would not be in sole charge of the hotel. Breakfast might be obtainable.

Peter shaved and dressed and went downstairs. On one of the landings he passed a girl who was listlessly operating a vacuum-cleaner on the pink carpet. A staff of sorts seemed to be assembling.

In the hall below he found Adrian Rolfe, who was very spruce in his green corduroy suit with a fresh frilled shirt of an apricot colour, but who was standing plucking at his lower lip and looking helpless.

'I've been wandering around here for about a quarter of an hour,' he said, 'and I can *smell* breakfast. Somewhere someone is cooking bacon. But I can't find any tables laid for us anywhere, and there seems to be no heating in the whole building.'

'Suppose we follow the scent,' Peter said. 'Assuming it leads to the kitchen,

129

we'll see if we can get some attention.'

Turning around, sniffing, he set off in the direction from which the savoury smell of the bacon was coming.

They found a kitchen with Anna standing at the stove, singing softly to herself, the pleasant sound of it mingling with the sizzling of the bacon in the frying pan.

'You want your breakfast, isn't it?' she said, looking round with the misleading coy look that came from the malformation of her shoulder. 'Go in the dining-room, I bring it in a minute.'

By the dining-room Peter supposed that she meant the big room where the writers' discussion had been held the evening before. Going out to it through the small bar, he and Rolfe settled themselves at one of the bare tables which had been replaced in the space occupied by the chairs for the audience the evening before, and waited hopefully.

Their breakfast did not arrive in a minute. It was about a quarter of an hour before the girl who had been using the vacuum-cleaner appeared with a tablecloth and a handful of knives and forks and asked if they wanted tea or coffee. Then after about another ten minutes Anna came with some crockery for them and two plates of bacon and eggs.

'You go today or stay another night?' she asked.

'I haven't decided,' Peter answered. 'I'll let you know presently.'

'So will I,' Rolfe said.

'The Swan in Sisslebridge is a very comfortable hotel,' she said. 'More comfortable than here. You have private bathrooms and very good service. Here we are too far out to keep a staff. We cannot give the service I would like.'

'I'll think about it and tell you,' Peter promised.

When she had left them Rolfe remarked, 'It would seem she wants rid of us.'

'Well, I suppose it's a bit of a nuisance having to keep the place ticking over for just two visitors,' Peter said. 'It can't pay them to have us here. But the place puzzles me. I can't understand why it's been allowed to run down as it has.'

'Are you staying on, do you think?' Rolfe asked.

'I'm not really sure. I thought I'd go over to Grey Gables to find out if there's any news of Dan, then make up my mind what to do.'

'I'll do the same, if you don't mind. Though if there isn't any news...' Rolfe paused and seemed to be giving all his attention to his fried egg.

'Well?' Peter said.

'Well, suppose all those people have decided to say nothing to the police, what should we do? Do we leave it at that, or would you say it's my duty to go to them with that last letter I had from Dan? The one I told you about. The one that shows he went in fear of his life.'

Peter became very still. A forkful of bacon and egg remained stationary, half-way to his mouth. Then, with deliberation, he raised it the rest of the way. But he found it extraordinarily difficult to swallow. Something constricted his throat.

A gleam of amusement showed on Rolfe's calm face.

132

It steadied Peter. He managed to swallow.

'I'd be very careful about showing that letter to anyone,' he said. 'You might find you were doing what I believe is called publishing a libel.'

'I'd thought of that,' Rolfe answered. 'But one sometimes has to take certain risks. However, I'll promise not to do anything in a hurry, if that will reassure you. Now suppose we go over to the house to see if there's any news.'

Peter nodded and they finished their breakfast, then set off down the drive together.

CHAPTER VI

At the gate they turned to the left, crossed the road and walked the twenty yards to the gate of Grey Gables. The road at that point curved to the left, changing to a narrow lane overhung by high hedges. A dripping sound came from under the hazels and hawthorns as moisture trickled from their bare twigs into the puddles on the muddy ground. There were clumps of primroses here and there along the bottoms of the hedgerows, looking fresh and lovely and beautifully undamaged by the hours of downpour.

They met Gina in the drive up to the grey stone house. It was even bigger than Peter had realized in the darkness, standing with a bleak, graceless solidity in the midst of a tangled, neglected garden. The garden had once, he could see, been laid out with unimaginative formality, but it had been allowed to run to seed, which perhaps had improved it. Around it there were empty meadows, which, Peter supposed, belonged to the house. If they did, Dan Braile must own a sizeable piece of land.

In the distance towards Sisslebridge, beyond a grove of larches which were tinged with their first brilliant spring greenery, the tops of some roofs appeared. The house was not nearly as isolated as Peter had gathered from everything that Kate Rowley had told him about it, and as he had thought in the dusk the evening before. Lingstead's development was creeping nearer.

'I was coming to find you,' Gina said. She was in the black trouser suit that she had worn the evening before and a sheepskin jacket. She spoke listlessly and her face was tired. 'He hasn't come back.'

'Then they're going to the police, are they?' Peter said.

'Would you believe it, they can't make up their minds?' She turned back to the house with them. 'I think Walter wants to but Kate says we ought to give it a bit longer. They've changed sides. Yesterday it was Kate who wanted to go to the police and Walter who told her not to lose her head. I don't believe those two care about anything but being on opposite sides.'

'What about your mother?' Peter asked.

'Oh, you know what she's like,' Gina said. 'She hasn't any opinions of her own. She just sits and moans, "We should never have done it!" Gone to that show yesterday evening, you know, and left Dan by himself. And Juliet's busy writing a short story she's just thought of and doesn't give a damn. And the Patons are out, searching again by daylight, and Miss Thorpe sits and knits. And I—I simply don't know what to do. I've been out searching too, but it's been no use. I think if it weren't for Mother, I'd just pack up and go home. I can't do any good here.'

'Tell me, Miss Marston,' Adrian Rolfe said, 'if Mr Braile wasn't really as ill as he seemed to be and last night simply wanted to get away from you all for a while, where do you think he'd have gone?'

Gina shrugged her shoulders. 'Perhaps to London. He's got a little flat there. Only I honestly don't think he could have done it. He *is* ill, I'm quite sure of it. And anyway, he didn't take any money with him.'

'You can't be sure of that,' Rolfe said. 'He may be one of those people who keep a hidden hoard for emergencies. Even his wife might not have known about it. And I remember someone saying he took a waterproof and an umbrella and gum-boots. This flat of his, where is it?'

'Near Parliament Hill Fields. But I tell you, he could never have got there. He'd have collapsed on the way. He couldn't even have got to Sisslebridge. He'd have had to walk all the way to the main road, which is at least a mile, then he'd have had to wait for a bus and there are very few of them in the evening.'

'Hasn't he any friends hereabouts whom he could have telephoned and who'd have come to fetch him?'

'Kate and Walter have been telephoning everyone they can think of, but no one's seen him.'

'Suppose he telephoned for a taxi.'

'Walter's telephoned both the taxi companies in Sisslebridge and neither sent a car out here yesterday evening after the one that brought Peter.' She frowned at Rolfe. 'They aren't utter fools in there, you know. After their fashion they're doing their best, only they're in a muddle.'

He returned her frown with one of his charming smiles. 'I'm sorry, I'm the fool. But I only wanted to help. It's meant so much to me, the thought of meeting Dan.'

The smile had some effect, for she gave a small smile back.

'Well, come inside,' she said, 'and see if you can think of anything else we can do.'

She took them through the austere white emptiness of the hall to the sitting-room.

The scene was curiously like the scene that Peter and Rolfe had left behind them the evening before, though Kate, instead of being dressed in shimmering red, was in dark-blue slacks and a heavy sweater and looked as if she had forgotten to comb her hair that morning. Also the Patons were not there. Juliet was sitting at a table, bent over it with an arm flung out as if to conceal what she was doing, and was writing something very fast. Walter Weldon was standing on the hearthrug with his back to the fire, polishing his spectacles, with his crumpled-looking features screwed up tightly as if against the light falling on his face now without the defence of his glasses. Helen, in a quilted dressing-gown, was sitting on a low stool with her arms clasped round her knees and her chin digging into them, her face empty and her eyelids red and swollen. Alice Thorpe was sitting by the fire, knitting. It would have been easy to believe that they had all spent the night like that.

Kate, seeing Peter, gave him one of her close embraces, her body hard against his. She only glanced at Rolfe indifferently.

'Gina will have told you, we've still heard nothing,' she said.

'What are you going to do about it?' Peter asked.

Walter put his spectacles on again. They

took away a lost look that he had had without them.

'I'm afraid we find ourselves hopelessly inadequate to cope with the situation,' he said. 'It's natural that we shouldn't want to go to the police. The fact that Dan got dressed and took his umbrella and so on makes it almost certain that he went away voluntarily. And though he's very well liked in the neighbourhood, he's regarded, I think, as a rather eccentric character. I'm afraid the police may simply be indifferent to his disappearance, or even suspect that the whole aim of it is to attract attention, get into the newspapers, get some publicity. In spite of that, however, I'm for calling them in.'

Remembering his own thoughts of the evening before, Peter said, 'I don't want to be offensive, but is there any possibility that that's actually the explanation of what's happened?'

Kate gave a snort of derision. 'That's the one thing on which Walter and I agree, that it's simply not in Dan's nature to think of a thing like that. But what other people who don't know him are going to think... People are so malicious and the more genuine you are, the less you're influenced by current materialistic values, which are the only ones they really understand, the more suspicious they are that you must be a fake. I realize we may have to go to the police in the end, but I don't think we should rush to do it before we're absolutely sure it's necessary.'

'What d'you call being absolutely sure?' Walter demanded. 'Finding his dead body in a ditch?'

'I suppose I mean I just think we ought to wait a bit longer,' Kate replied. 'And perhaps... Oh, of course I know what I'd really like to do, though the rest of you may not agree. I'd like to consult Max. He's got such a wonderfully clear brain—hasn't he, Peter? If we told him everything that's happened, don't you think he might be able to advise us?'

'By all means,' Walter said before Peter could answer. 'I agree that Max might be very useful. So ring him up. Get him down here. Anything you like, so long as it stops this sitting around, talking uselessly.'

'What do you think, Peter, about consulting Max?' Kate asked.

'I think it's an extremely good idea,' he answered.

'The only trouble is,' she said, 'he might not be able to get away from the office in the middle of the week. But if you went up and told him everything...' She broke off as the Patons came in. Their arms were entwined as usual and there was something oddly similar on their two very different faces, a look of alertness and excitement. Kate responded to it at once and exclaimed, 'Oh God, don't tell us you've found something!'

'No,' Cliff said, 'nothing positive. But we've had an idea and we've been talking it over and we're certain it's the only explanation of what's happened. It's absolutely obvious once you think of it. Don't you see, Dan's been kidnapped?'

'Oh!...' It was a high, thin wail from Helen. She hid her face on her knees and began to rock to and fro. 'No, no, not kidnapped, no!'

Kate stared hard at the Patons. 'Some mothers do have 'em,' she said drily. 'Did you think that bright idea of yours would make Helen feel better?'

Both the Patons reddened.

'I'm sorry,' Cliff muttered. 'We shouldn't have blurted it out like that. Crazy thing to do. We should have spoken to you privately. It's just that we've been walking round the place again this morning and it's obvious that Dan was taken away by somebody. The simple fact is, he couldn't have got away alone. We went down the hill towards Sisslebridge and we found the water across the road is still quite deep. Last night it would have been a river. And even if he could have waded through it, he'd have had quite a long walk before he could have got a bus or a lift in a car. And we're all sure, aren't we, that he wasn't well enough for that? Well, then Rosie and I went up the other way along the lane, and there isn't a single house till you get to that hamlet, Burley's End, which is a good two miles away. And we went from house to house there, asking if anyone had seen Dan—'

'You did *what?*' Walter's face flamed. 'You took it on yourselves, without consulting any of us, to tell all those people that Dan's gone missing?'

'Oh, Walter,' Juliet said, raising her head and speaking irritably, 'do you have to shout so loud? I've quite forgotten what I was just going to write.'

'Why can't you work in our room, if you must?' he demanded. 'If you'd any sort of heart you wouldn't be writing at all.'

'That's where you're wrong,' she said. 'I'm writing because I'm so afraid of what I'd feel if I didn't.' She sank her head into the crook of her arm again and her pen moved onward.

Helen lifted her head. Her eyes had an unnatural staring look.

'But why did you say kidnapped?' she asked the Patons. 'Why should anyone kidnap Dan?'

Cliff Paton shifted from one foot to the other. 'Well, perhaps we were going too fast. But a famous man like Dan, living in a big house like this—they may have taken for granted he was very rich. And kidnapping's getting so common nowadays. I'm so sorry if I frightened you, Helen, but I do honestly think it's a possibility we ought to consider.'

'How would kidnappers have known that just last night Dan would be alone?' Kate asked. 'You aren't suggesting that anyone here—one of us—gave them the information?' But as she said it her forehead wrinkled and she looked with a new curiosity at Adrian Rolfe.

'They could have heard it from anyone in the Arts League,' Cliff replied. 'They'd all have known Dan had cancelled going to the meeting.'

'If you're right...' Kate began thoughtfully, then paused, biting on a knuckle. 'I do wish Max was here,' she went on. 'This possibility—I suppose we can't simply say it's nonsense—I suppose it really means we've got to go to the police.'

'The very opposite,' Walter said sharply. 'If we take this idea seriously for a moment, the only thing to do is wait till the kidnappers get in touch with us with their instructions. Then we can decide whether to take the police into our confidence or not.'

'But we've no money!' Helen's voice went up into a muted kind of scream. 'You know we haven't. Dan's books only make us just enough to get by. You all pay your share when you stay here. We've never saved anything. We've got this house, that's all. Dan bought it for a song years ago before prices started rocketing and it was crumbling with dry rot which we've put right only little by little. But it isn't mine, it's Dan's. I can't sell it for him. So if they ring up and say they want money, what are we going to do?'

Gina, who had been sitting silently on the arm of a chair, suddenly sprang to her feet.

'I've never heard such nonsense!' she cried. 'Nobody's kidnapped Dan. And if the rest of you won't make up your minds what to do, I'll make up mine. I'm going to the police. I'm going now. Whatever the truth is, Dan's very ill and we've got to find him.'

She walked out of the room.

Helen shot to her feet and looked as if she was going to run after her, but Walter caught her by the arm. He drew her close to him.

'Peter,' he said, 'quick, go after her, stop her, will you? Talk to her. She'll listen to you.'

'If that girl thinks she's doing the right thing, why not let her?' Rolfe said.

'This has nothing to do with you,' Walter told him harshly. 'Anyway, it isn't the right thing, because her mother doesn't want it—do you, Helen?' He looked into her face, his protective arm still round her.

She gave a quick shake of her head.

'And she's the one who's got the right to say what should be done,' Walter said. 'Peter, will you go after Gina?'

Peter gave a dubious nod and said, 'All right, I'll see what I can do.'

He started off.

When he emerged from the house he saw Gina halfway down the drive already. He shouted after her. She took no notice. He shouted again and she stopped and looked round. When she saw who it was she waited for him. Hurrying to catch up with her, it annoyed him to discover that Rolfe had followed him out and was keeping up with him. Just then Peter wanted Gina to himself.

'You needn't try to make me change my mind,' she said as they joined her. 'No one's done anything but talk since last night. It's time somebody did something.'

'I agree,' Peter said. 'It's just a question of what, and I've got some ideas about that myself. Suppose we go to the Manor House and have a drink, if we can persuade anyone to open the bar, and I'll tell you what's occurred to me.'

She gave him a suspicious look. 'You're trying to get round me.'

'Yes,' he admitted. 'But I'll tell you what I'll do. If you don't like my idea I'll go to the police with you. I suppose you mean the police in Sisslebridge.'

She nodded. 'But I don't need a bodyguard, thank you, or anyone to speak for me.'

'Would there be any harm in spending half an hour over a drink and listening to my idea?' Peter asked.

'All right,' she said reluctantly and they started to walk on towards the hotel. 'But if we give in to that crowd's delaying tactics any longer we'll never get anywhere.'

'Delaying tactics?' Rolfe said. 'You think it's deliberate?'

'Of course it is! At least it is on Walter's part. Haven't you noticed that whatever Kate says, he takes the opposite side? And the result's just more talk, talk, talk. And when the Patons came in with that ridiculous idea of theirs about kidnapping, he seized on it as an excuse for doing nothing.'

'But why should he do that, apart from being genuinely uncertain what it's best to do?' Peter asked.

'Haven't you got eyes?'

'Perhaps I haven't. What is it I haven't seen?'

'That he's in love with Mother. I believe he has been for a long time but he's only just begun to let it show. He doesn't mind our seeing how much he quarrels with Juliet and he's always touching Mother and putting his arms around her and standing up for her. And you see, I think that may mean I was absolutely wrong last night when I told you Dan's trouble was cancer or an ulcer. And I don't think it's gastric 'flu or hysteria either. I think he was right about what's wrong with him. I think he's been poisoned.'

'By Weldon?' Rolfe asked.

'Of course.'

'That's quite an accusation,' Peter said sombrely.

They crossed the road and started up the drive to the hotel. Gina held herself very erect, with a cold, closed look on her face.

Before they reached the porch, Rolfe said, 'You'll realize that if you make the police believe that, they'll assume your mother's involved.'

'Not when they meet her,' Gina said. 'How could anyone suspect her of anything?'

'Who's been preparing Dan's food?' Peter asked.

'All of us, taking it in turns. Sometimes it was Mother, sometimes Kate, sometimes I did it, sometimes it was even Juliet, though it always had to be scrambled eggs when it was her turn. But Walter always carried the tray upstairs and of course nobody watched him. He could easily have scattered some arsenic, or whatever it was, into the soup or the coffee.'

'And you believe this could go on without your mother having even a suspicion of it?' Rolfe said. 'After all, she must have realized Weldon's in love with her.'

'Of course I believe it.'

'Well, I assure you the police aren't going to,' he said. 'However obviously innocent your mother may seem to you, the police are going to realize that she isn't a strong character and might easily be dominated by a stronger one, like Weldon. That's a common pattern in murder. Someone who doesn't really understand what's happening is manipulated by someone who's ruthless and brutal. So unless you don't mind the idea of getting your mother into trouble,

I'd really think very carefully before you rush off to them.'

Gina stood still. 'What do you mean— unless I don't *mind* getting my mother into trouble. Of course I do.'

'Well, daughters aren't always devoted to mothers and the police know that, even if they've never heard of Electra.'

Gina grasped Peter's arm. 'Do I have to listen to that sort of thing?'

'All you have to do is come inside and have a drink and listen to me,' he answered. He looked at Rolfe. 'You can join us if you don't keep needling the girl. I want to keep her as rational as possible.'

'What else was I trying to do myself?' Rolfe asked. 'I was only pointing out the dangers of what she was proposing to do.'

'I thought perhaps you were trying to goad her—remembering that last letter of Dan's—into some sort of self-betrayal. I shouldn't try that, if I were you.'

'Oh, but you're quite, quite wrong,' Rolfe said with a sunny smile. 'Now that I've met Gina I've realized that poor Dan can't have known what he was doing when he wrote that.'

Far from believing him, Peter gave him a warning scowl.

'What are you both talking about?' Gina asked, looking uncertainly from one to the other.

Peter put an arm round her shoulders. 'Nothing much. Now let's see if the bar's functioning, or if we've got to dig up Anna or someone from the nether regions.'

He drew Gina along the passage to the bar.

The grille over the counter had been raised, which implied that the bar was officially open, but there was no sign of anyone to attend to it. Knowing his way to the kitchen now, Peter went to it and found Anna there, sitting at a table drinking coffee with a stout woman in a white overall who, he supposed, was the hotel cook. But the coffee was probably of Anna's brewing, for it had a strongly continental aroma. Something savoury was cooking in the oven.

She looked round when she heard Peter

come in and said, 'You want a drink, isn't it?'

'Yes, please. And could you manage some lunch? There are three of us.'

'Sandwiches?' she suggested. 'Good sandwiches, cold beef, chicken, cheese, what you like, but we are not expecting anyone to lunch. We cook only for ourselves.'

'All right then, sandwiches,' Peter said.

'And a drink first, yes? I come.' She finished her coffee, got up and followed Peter to the bar.

Gina and Rolfe had sat down at one of the small round tables, but as soon as Anna appeared Rolfe jumped up and insisted on buying the drinks. Leaning against the bar as she poured them out, he said, 'Anna, will you tell me something? Something I've got very curious about. Have Lingstead's bought this hotel?'

'Oh yes,' she answered, 'three months ago they buy it. I mean, three months ago everything is agreed. They talk about it with Mr Danby six months, a year before that. And a few days ago everything is signed. It is all a question of planning permission. Now they have it they build ten, twelve houses on the land here. And the hotel they turn into a club for their workers and I am to be housekeeper. It is all very good.'

'So that's why the hotel is—well, like it is,' Rolfe said.

'Ach, the hotel!' She laughed. 'It is terrible, I know that. When Mr Danby buys it two years ago he builds on this bar and the fine new dining-room and says, "I will have a real good class restaurant here." And everywhere else, he says, he will make new when he can afford it. He will make a swimming pool and it will be a fine new holiday hotel. Then Lingstead's come and soon they make him offers. So he spends no more on the hotel and he buys a villa in Spain with the great sum of money he gets and now, next week, the builders come and the hotel is closed and I stay at home till the work is finished and the club opens. There will be a lot of life then, it is all very good. But I tell you, if you want to stay on in Sisslebridge, the Swan is a very good hotel. I have worked there before I come here. Is clean, comfortable, good food.'

'The sum of money Mr Danby got from Lingstead's,' Rolfe said, 'it was a very large sum, was it?'

'I have heard rumours they pay him eighty thousand,' she replied. 'Some people say more. I think it is more, but he never told me. He slaps his pocket and chuckles. He is a very happy man.'

'I see.' Rolfe picked up the three drinks and brought them across to the table where Gina and Peter were sitting.

Peter saw too. He saw a number of things, among which was the fact that Adrian Rolfe, in spite of his youth, his frilly shirts and disarming beauty, which made it difficult to take him seriously, was a very shrewd character. He had just made sure that Grey Gables was a very valuable property, for it was certainly worth a great deal more than the Manor House, because it had far more land, on which far more than ten or twelve houses could be built.

But would Dan sell it?

It seemed certain that Lingstead's would

have approached him before they approached Mr Danby. So he must already have refused their offer. Yet as his quiet home became encircled by Lingstead's rapidly expanding empire, would it retain any charm for him? Soon, in whatever direction he looked, he would see roofs showing above the treetops. The quiet lane to his gate would be busy with cars. The children of the families who came to live in the new houses would steal his fruit, perhaps trample his flowers and commit the other acts of vandalism common to the adolescent. The peace that he needed for himself and that he liked to share with others would be lost for ever.

But what connection could this have with his disappearance?

None that Peter could think of, unless one permitted oneself a very ugly thought. The thought that someone, and it could only be Helen because she was the only one who would benefit, wanted the money that Dan had refused so much more than she wanted Dan that she had been slowly poisoning him. And Dan, having guessed it, had seized the first chance that he had had to bolt.

Of course, if Gina was right that there was something between Helen and Walter Weldon, it could have been Walter who had been administering the poison. And if that happened to be so, Peter suddenly thought, what odds would anyone give on Juliet's chances of survival? What was Juliet herself thinking about that at the moment? Far more, very likely, than she was saying.

A prickle of cold ran up Peter's spine. He was letting his imagination get out of hand.

'Well, what's this idea of yours?' Gina asked him impatiently.

He replied, 'This morning you said that if Dan could get away, he'd probably go to his flat in London. Don't you think that's perhaps what he's done?'

She frowned. 'How could he possibly have got there?'

'Something Paton said gave me an idea,' Peter answered. 'He talked of how far Dan would have to go before he could have caught a bus or got a lift in a car. But suppose in fact he got a lift very quickly. Suppose he managed to dress himself and get out into the road just about the time the meeting in the hotel was breaking up. There'd have been lots of cars going back to Sisslebridge along the lane. And a good many people probably knew Dan. If he waved, someone would have stopped and very likely taken him to the station.'

'I see.' Gina rolled a lock of her fair hair round and round one finger. 'And if he'd a little money on him, and we can't be sure he hadn't, he could have got a ticket... Yes, I think he'd have gone to the flat.'

'If he was strong enough to do that.'

'Yes, and I don't truly think he was.'

'All the same, before we talk any more of going to the police, wouldn't it be best to go there and make sure?'

'Perhaps it would,' she said musingly.

'And if we don't find him, I could do what Kate suggested, go and see Max.'

'Right,' Adrian Rolfe said briskly. 'I'll drive the two of you up to London this afternoon.'

CHAPTER VII

Peter sat in the back of the car, Gina in the seat beside Adrian Rolfe.

Peter felt drowsy, the result of not having slept well the night before and of having had too much pressure of other people's problems upon him. The fact that he saw no hope of getting ahead with his work probably for another day or two filled him with what he knew was a not quite rational anxiety. There was actually no need for desperate haste. But when he was interrupted in his writing for longer than he had planned he often had the feeling that it would be impossible for him ever to take it up again, that the thread had been irreparably broken, that everything that he had written up to that point would be wasted and that the time at which his next cheque would come in might become dangerously distant.

In the seats in front of him Gina and Rolfe started an argument. Peter listened to them on and off, but paid more attention to the shape of Gina's head, outlined against the windscreen, the sweep of her bright hair and the pleasant sound of her soft, light voice than to what she was saying. When he did attend to it, it struck him as rather solemn or boring. Was that what she was like with her own generation? Was that what they were all like with one another?

He heard her say, 'But I don't understand why you don't do any job at all. Doing nothing in particular must make life seem terribly empty.'

'Not nearly as empty as it would be if I had to do almost any job I can think of,' Rolfe answered.

'Well, of course if you don't need money there's no reason why you should take it out of the mouths of the people who do,' Gina said, 'but don't you ever want to do something useful?'

'Not particularly.'

'Haven't you got any ambitions?'

161

'Do you think I ought to have? Do you like ambitious people?'

'Not much, but I do like useful people.'

'You don't mean you can see me taking up social work?'

'Oh, there are all kinds of ways of being useful.'

'Like driving you to London, for instance.'

'No, that's being—well, just good-natured, though I really think you're doing it from curiosity.'

Rolfe laughed. 'That isn't kind. I suppose what you want me to do is something creative. Writing, painting, acting. Unfortunately I've absolutely no talents.'

'How d'you know if you haven't tried?'

'But I have tried—almost everything. I've even thought that to justify my existence I might go off into darkest Africa and find some poor blacks who wouldn't mind my trying to teach them a lot of useless things.'

'I don't believe that thought ever crossed your mind. Anyway, it's out of date, isn't it? Of course, you might have taught

162

them something like modern methods of agriculture.'

'I don't know anything about agriculture, ancient or modern.'

She was silent. She was not used, Peter guessed, to being even mildly teased. She was too used to an atmosphere of high seriousness.

After a pause she said, 'You and I don't agree about many things, do we? Take Dan, for instance. You're one of his hero-worshippers. But I think he's a terrible man. Yes, really terrible. He only uses other people, he doesn't care for them. You'll find he uses you when you get to know him. And you'll probably love it. A lot of people do. It's extraordinary how many people enjoy being trampled on, if it's done in a particular way.'

She was thinking, Peter supposed, of her mother.

Rolfe took his eyes off the road ahead for a moment to give her a brief glance.

'You said you like people who are useful,' he said. 'Isn't it a way of being useful to let someone like Daniel Braile

163

trample on you, if that's what he needs?'

'Because he's a genius? Only I don't think he is a genius, you see. I know he's been rediscovered recently, but I think in another ten years no one will read him.'

'But perhaps in another fifty they will.'

'I don't worry much about what people are going to say in fifty years' time.'

'But think, you'll be only seventy and you'll be able to say to your admirers, "When I was a young girl I used to be a *very* intimate friend of Daniel Braile. The things I could tell you about him..." And they'll listen spell-bound.'

'I don't suppose I shall have admirers when I'm seventy,' she said. 'But in any case, I shouldn't talk about Dan. I should be doing my best to forget him. When I think of what he did to us...'

'To your family?'

There was a slight change in Rolfe's tone that alerted Peter. He did his best to throw off his drowsiness and pay attention to what the two in front of him were saying. Suddenly they seemed to him extremely young and close to one another because of it, even if in a sense they were opponents. It gave him a sense of middle-aged decay from which he suffered only very occasionally. Normally he found forty a most satisfactory age to be and would not have gone back to the insecurity and vulnerability of youth for anything in the world.

'Of course,' Gina answered. 'But I know what you'll say. He couldn't have broken up our home if my mother hadn't wanted it. I've never really known how it happened. I was only thirteen.'

'Do you think your mother has ever wanted to go back to your father?'

She seemed startled. 'But he's married again.'

'Do second marriages always stick better than first ones?'

'I—I never thought about it,' she said.

'Are you fond of your stepmother?'

'Yes, she's very sweet. She's pretty and—sort of uncomplicated. And very affectionate. I think she and my father are very happy together.'

'But wouldn't you be happier if your

mother and father came together again?'

Peter decided that it was time to intervene. Gina seemed wholly unconscious of the fact that she was being pumped. Pumped, as she could not know, by a man whose idol had told him that she was a poisoner.

'I've just thought of something,' Peter said. 'Suppose Dan's in the flat but doesn't happen to feel like opening the door to us, which is quite likely, after all, how do we find out if he's there.'

'It's all right, I've got a key,' Gina said.

'Then you stay in the flat yourself sometimes, do you?' Rolfe asked.

'Never, as a matter of fact. Dan gave me the key and told me to use the place any time I wanted to, but I've never needed it. I live with my father, who's got a house in Richmond.'

'But it was quite generous of Dan, wasn't it, to give you a key? He may have thought you might like to get away on your own sometimes, or even have somewhere to go with a boy-friend.'

166

She pounded with her fists on her knees. 'Yes, yes, it was generous. I've never said anything against Dan's generosity. I suppose he's tried very hard to make me like him and it's all my fault that I can't. Perhaps if I'd tried harder I'd have managed it. Only I haven't much wanted to try. But you're quite wrong if you think he ever dreamt that I might take a boy-friend to his blessed flat. He's a fearful old puritan. You should hear the things he says about the present-day young. He's utterly intolerant and doesn't understand the first thing about us. I simply can't think how his novels were ever thought daring. One of them nearly got banned, didn't it? It strikes me as wildly ridiculous. They're all unspeakably proper.'

'It was quite a long time ago that that happened,' Rolfe said. 'And he did break new ground and said a lot of things that hadn't been said before. You shouldn't underrate him. About this flat of his, does he use it often?'

'I don't really know,' Gina replied. 'I don't see much of him. I stay with them at Grey Gables about twice a year, and sometimes when Mother comes to London on her own we meet and have a meal together and she stays in the flat then. But if Dan's up on his own he and I don't think of meeting, so I don't know how often he comes. Why do you want to know?'

'I suppose I'm just wondering what kind of place the flat will turn out to be,' Rolfe said. 'Will it be a bit less bleak than that mansion of his? I admit it gave me a shock. I don't understand how your mother puts up with it.'

'It wouldn't do her much good not to,' Gina said. 'He'll sometimes take opposition from other people, but never from her. He goes into deadly silent sulks if she dares to stand up to him the least little bit, and the treatment breaks her to pieces. After a few days of it she just grovels to him to forgive her. It's horrible to watch. But sometimes I think it's almost like a kind of game that she enjoys as much as he does. Or used to. I've thought recently she's been getting tired of it.'

'And that would please you,' Rolfe said, 'if she hadn't fallen in love with Weldon.'

She turned her head quickly to look at him. She seemed about to break out with something violent, but Peter could see her force herself to hold it in. Sinking down in her seat, she said nothing. One or two efforts by Rolfe to start her talking again were answered by monosyllables and the rest of the drive to Dan Braile's London flat was almost in silence.

The flat was in a converted Victorian house which stood in a small garden surrounded by laurels. A neat asphalt walk led up to the entrance. There was a row of six bells beside the door, with a card beside each bell. Daniel Braile's name was on the third from the bottom.

Peter was putting out his finger to press the bell when Gina stopped him.

'He could look out of the window and see us here and perhaps bolt down the fire-escape, if that's the sort of mood he's in,' she said. 'Let's go straight up.'

She went in quickly at the door and started up the staircase.

On the second landing she paused and put a finger to her lips.

Distinctly from behind the door there came the sound of a typewriter.

Rolfe's face showed excitement. 'We've caught him after all. I never believed for a moment we were going to. Where's your key? Let's go straight in.'

Gina grinned. Taking a key out of her handbag, she slid it quietly into the lock, turned it quickly and thrust the door open.

Juliet Weldon, who was sitting at a table facing them in the large room that they entered, looked up from the typewriter at which she was working and said without much interest, 'So you thought of this too. No good, my dears, not a sign of him.'

Gina advanced a few steps towards her. The room was a light, bright place, yet curiously like the sitting-room at Grey Gables, shabby, austere, rather chilling.

'What are you doing here?' Gina asked brusquely.

'The same as you,' Juliet answered, pushing her chair back from the table and standing up languidly. She left a sheet of paper in the typewriter. 'Checking if he'd come here before we finally decided to go to the police.'

'How did you get in?'

'Helen gave me her key. She didn't come herself, of course, in case he turned up at home. And you hadn't told me you meant to come. If you had, you could have saved me the drive.'

Gina went forward to look at the sheet of paper that Juliet had left in the typewriter.

'A note for Dan,' she said.

Juliet stretched and yawned. She was in her usual jeans and anorak, and with her page-boy bob curling in at her neck she looked very young except for something almost withered in her pallid face.

'Yes, I've been sitting here,' she said, 'wondering what the hell I was supposed to do, stay here indefinitely on the chance that he might still turn up, or go back to the others. Then I thought I could leave a note for him and go. I've been getting bloody bored.'

Gina read the note aloud. ' "Don't be

a fool, Dan, this isn't going to get you anywhere. Stay here if you want to, but at least telephone, or they'll put the police on your tracks, if they haven't done it already. I sympathize with you, of course, but what you've done is idiocy. J." '

She looked at Juliet. 'I don't understand it.'

'That's all right,' Juliet said. 'Dan will.'

Peter went to the typewriter and read the note over Gina's shoulder.

'What does it mean—"this isn't going to get you anywhere"?' he asked.

'I don't see any need to explain it,' Juliet answered.

'It's open to misinterpretation.'

'Not by Dan.'

'You must be very sure you know why he's vanished then.'

She smiled. It gave an unaccustomed expression to her rather vacant face, lighting it up with a touch of cruelty.

'I've got eyes,' she said.

'Our impression,' Rolfe said, 'is that Dan vanished because he believed someone at Grey Gables was trying to poison him.

Suppose he was right, what you've written sounds almost like a threat that you'll get him in the end whatever he does.' He turned to Peter. 'Isn't that what you meant by misinterpretation?'

Peter nodded.

Juliet strolled to a chair and dropped into it. She felt in a pocket of her anorak for a packet of cigarettes, put one in her mouth and lit it. As she breathed out smoke her sharp little smile still lingered.

'Dan's never believed he was being poisoned,' she said.

'But he does. I've got it in writing,' Rolfe said with a new note of aggression in his voice.

Juliet moved her head to look at him. Her smile held pity and mockery.

'Ah, one of those famous letters he wrote you,' she said. 'A very imaginative writer, Dan. Poor man, he never could resist drama.'

'I never believed Dan thought he was being poisoned until today,' Gina said. 'I thought he was just afraid to face what was really the matter with him. After all, poison's a thing you can run away from. You can't run away from cancer.'

'Cancer?' Juliet said and laughed, an unusual reaction to the mention of that word. 'You really thought he had cancer?'

'I don't know—not any more,' Gina answered. 'What did you mean about his not believing he was being poisoned?'

'For God's sake, look at what's actually happened,' Juliet said. 'And face the fact that Dan intended it all to happen. Think of how we're all reacting and realize we're doing just what he wanted. First we get worried because he's ill and after that because just perhaps he's right about the poison and we start—oh yes, we do—getting a little suspicious of one another, in case there's a murderer amongst us. But we play it down because after all we're all old friends, aren't we? We trust each other. Don't we just! However, the way we take things doesn't please Dan, so he goes a step further and vanishes. And then we really begin to worry. But do we call in the police, like reasonable people? No, we don't, because in spite of the beautiful trust we have in one another, we think that possibly—just, just possibly—Dan was telling the truth all along and one of us is a poisoner and if we can't find him on our own we'll be involved in all the horrors of a criminal scandal.'

Peter sat down at the typewriter, rolled out the sheet of paper that Juliet had left in it, crumpled it, tossed it into a waste-paper basket and rolled a fresh sheet in.

Juliet sat upright in her chair. 'Why did you do that?' she asked angrily.

'Because you don't believe a word you've been saying,' he answered. 'It was a good idea to leave a message for Dan, but something quite simple will be much the best.' He began to pick out the keys, reading aloud what he was writing. ' "Dan—if you see this, please telephone Helen at once and let her know you're all right. We're all very worried." How shall I sign it?'

'Helen? Telephone Helen?' Juliet cried. Then all of a sudden she began to laugh hysterically. She covered her face with her hands, leant forward till her chin was touching her knees and let out scream after scream of laughter. Her thin body shook all over. The cigarette that she had been smoking slid out of her fingers on to the carpet and smouldered there.

Rolfe picked it up and stubbed it out in the empty fireplace.

The two men and Gina watched Juliet for a moment, hoping for the paroxysm to pass of itself, but her laugher only grew louder and tears began to trickle through her fingers.

Peter crossed to her side, grasped her by the shoulder, jerked her upright and shook her hard.

'Stop it, Juliet—you can,' he said. 'This isn't like you.'

'What do you know about me?' she gasped. But her laugher degenerated abruptly into violent hiccups. 'Haven't you ever seen me make a scene before? How lucky you are! If I was at home, alone with Walter, I could keep it up for hours. Only I'm never alone at home with Walter nowadays. He's too afraid of me. So we're always at Grey Gables.'

Rolfe began to wander round the room, looking in cupboards.

'I wonder if there's anything to drink in this place,' he said. 'Brandy? Whisky?'

'Try the kitchen,' Gina suggested.

He disappeared into the kitchen.

Peter tugged at his chin, looking down at Juliet.

'I suppose I know what this is all about,' he said. 'You think Walter and Helen are in love with one another, and that Dan thinks so too, and he's been poisoning himself, or pretending to, to give them a fright and make them distrust one another. And then, when that didn't seem to be working, he disappeared, so that they shouldn't be able to find out the truth about him, but would have to stop seeing each other in case his dead body turned up somewhere with arsenic in it and the motive of one or other or both would be a bit too obvious. That's it, isn't it, Juliet? In your message to Dan you told him that what he was doing wasn't going to get him anywhere, but that you sympathized with him.'

She did not answer. She was holding her breath and swallowing in an effort to control the hiccups. Her tears had stopped, though there were still damp smudges on her cheeks.

Rolfe reappeared from the kitchen.

'Here's some brandy,' he said and put a glass into her hand.

She made a face and swallowed it quickly. She still did not try to speak. Peter returned to the typewriter and looked down at what he had written.

'Actually there's no need to sign it, is there?' he said. 'If Dan ever comes here it won't really matter who came to look for him.'

Juliet gave a deep sigh. She was still very pale, but had regained control of herself.

'He won't come here,' she said. 'I told them he wouldn't, but they insisted someone had to make sure.'

'Why are you sure he won't come?' Peter asked. 'That message you wrote sounded as if you expected him to read it.'

'I did that just to pass the time. And I was thinking the whole thing out while

178

I wrote it. You're quite right, of course, about what I think. About Helen and Walter. And you're probably surprised at how much I care.'

'I think you're right about them,' Gina said. 'Half-right, anyway.'

Rolfe gave her a quick look, curious, alert. Peter realized that although the young man had arrived full of suspicion of her, intending to see her as evil, the girl herself with her strange eyes, her deep, intent gaze and her directness, had challenged him to search more deeply into her, in the hope perhaps of finding innocence.

'How much longer d'you mean to stay here, Juliet?' Peter asked.

She got a little staggeringly to her feet.

'I think I'll go now.'

'You're driving back?'

'Yes,' she said.

'You're all right to drive?'

'Quite all right, thank you. These moods I get, when they're over, they're over.' Drawing herself upright and lifting her head, she seemed to be visibly shredding the after-effects of her hysteria. But there was something profoundly disconsolate about her which made Peter follow her through the door and out on to the landing.

He put an arm round her shoulders.

'I'm sure you're wrong, Juliet. Walter isn't in love with Helen. You're the only woman he's ever cared about.'

He was not at all sure that he believed this, but he felt a sudden urge to comfort her.

She gave a downward-curving smile. 'I suppose that's meant well. It may even be true. It may only be Helen's money Walter's in love with—because, of course, if Dan dies and Helen sells Grey Gables, she'll get a quite impressive sum. Walter does so love money, because, poor darling, he's never had any. When he married me he thought I was going to be a successful writer. I'm such a disappointment to him.'

'But you *are* a successful writer. You're very, very good.'

'Not in the way he'd like, if you could get him ever to be honest about it. Well, never mind about that now. Are you staying in

London or going back to Sisslebridge?'

'I'll have to go back. I left my suitcase there. If I hadn't I think I'd just go home. I don't see what good I can do.'

'I'll see you later then.'

She gave him a light pat on the arm, as if comforting him for the fact that the comfort that he had tried to give her had been so unavailing, and ran lightly down the stairs.

Peter returned to the sitting-room.

He found Gina and Rolfe standing side by side at the window in silence. But in that silence and in the way they were standing there Peter thought that he perceived a new awareness of one another. They drew farther apart as he came in.

'What are your plans?' he asked. 'Do you want to go straight back to Sisslebridge?'

'What do you think we ought to do?' Gina asked.

'If you don't mind waiting for me and can find some way of filling in the time,' he said, 'there's something I'd like to do before I go back. I'd like to have a talk with Max Rowley.'

'Ah yes, you said that before, didn't you?' Gina said. 'I suppose it's a good idea. Max is such a funny little man, but he's brilliant, isn't he? He's sure to give us some good advice. We can come too, can't we?'

'I think I'd sooner have a talk with him on my own,' Peter said. 'Not necessarily a long one. Then we might meet for dinner and drive down to Sisslebridge afterwards.'

She agreed unwillingly and Rolfe suggested a restaurant where they could meet later. As the two of them left the room together Peter picked up Dan Braile's telephone and began to dial.

But it was not Max's number that he dialled. First he dialled Caroline's.

He heard the telephone ringing and ringing in her flat and he let it go on for so long that even if she had been in a bath she would have had time to answer it. So her flat was empty. She worked for an advertising firm, but normally she would be home by now. What was she doing with herself, he wondered with a good deal of exasperation, and felt a sudden craving for her company that took him by surprise. There was a lot to be said for maturity when you had been exposed for too long to the young. Even the very lovely and appealing young. Or was he saying that to himself only because he had seen how quickly Gina's interest in Rolfe had flared up? There was just enough antagonism between them to make their thoughts of one another exciting.

Putting the telephone down with a slight slam, Peter waiting a moment, picked it up again and this time dialled Max's number.

CHAPTER VIII

'I don't really understand what you think I can do for you, Peter,' Max said as he and Peter settled down on either side of the gas fire in the Rowley's small, cluttered sitting-room. 'If you just want me to listen while you talk, go ahead. But I'm no detective.'

He poured out whisky for them both. His sharp-boned, sombre face was attentive but slightly puzzled.

'Hasn't Kate told you what's happened?' Peter asked.

'Oh yes, Kate. On the telephone. As a matter of fact, only a little while before you telephoned yourself. She wants me to go down to Sisslebridge, which I told her I can't possibly do at the moment. Anyway, what use would I be?'

'You might pour cold water on some mounting hysteria. You're good at that.'

'Is that what you think it is—hysteria?'

'Well, what do you think yourself?'

'On the basis of what Kate told me, I couldn't possibly guess. I think it might be best if you forgot that Kate's been talking to me. Try telling me everything you can remember as if I hadn't heard anything at all. And let me make it plain I don't expect to be able to say anything helpful. But of course it's an intriguing problem and I'm rather itching to hear all the details. Flattered too at the idea that the wise man could help you solve it. Go ahead.'

'I was just remembering,' Peter said, leaning back in his chair and sipping his whisky, 'that a couple of nights ago you were saying you'd rather like to know someone who'd committed a particularly atrocious crime.'

'Was I really?' Max said. 'The things one says. If it came to the point, I'm sure I shouldn't like it at all. However, I suppose we all have ideas of that sort one time or another. We want to test ourselves. Find out what our own moralities, if any, are made of. But that's wandering from

185

the point, which seems to be that you're convinced an atrocious crime of some kind has been committed.'

'No, as a matter of fact, I'm not,' Peter said. 'I'm not sure that any crime has been committed yet.'

'Yet?'

Peter stirred uneasily. 'That's the trouble. I'm not sure that there's any reason to worry about what's happened so far. I may be wrong, of course. But I've a feeling of something working up... Still, that isn't the right way to begin. I'll try to stick to facts and not bother you with my impressions.'

'I shouldn't be surprised if the impressions would be the more valuable,' Max said. 'I shouldn't leave them out.'

'Well, of course it began, as far as I was concerned, with Kate's telephone call to me here.'

Max nodded.

'And you remember I refused to go to Grey Gables.'

'Yes.'

'Then Gina rang me at home...'

From that point Peter went on, step by step, as well as he could remember it, with all that had happened since he had arrived at the Manor House Hotel.

Max hardly interrupted him. From time to time he nodded or asked a question. Once he refilled Peter's glass. Most of Max's questions, it interested Peter to notice, concerned the value of Dan Braile's property. That was the lawyer in Max coming out, Peter thought. The small man with his austerely handsome face seemed to find money the only motive for crime that needed to be taken seriously.

Once or twice Max nodded his head as Peter tried to elucidate his own feelings about Dan Braile and the people at Grey Gables, ending with describing the scene with Juliet that had just occurred in Dan's London flat. But when Peter finished Max only sat there in silence, thinking hard, it appeared, but finding nothing to say.

As the silence lengthened out Peter began to wonder why he had come. What had made him think that Max, hearing the whole story like this at second hand, could help?

At last Max coughed apologetically and said, 'Sorry. My thoughts were straying. That's quite a lot you've told me. I wonder, would you find it quite intolerable to go over the whole thing again?'

'Good God, you sound like a policeman,' Peter said. 'Asking one to repeat oneself— isn't that what they do when they're trying to get a suspect to trip himself up?'

'You aren't a suspect and I don't want to trip you up. It's only that now I've got a general idea of things, I might understand the significance of some of the details rather better if you could face telling me the story a second time.'

'All right then.'

Peter started again. He tried to tell the story in as nearly the same words as before as he could, though he was aware that at times he contracted the first version and at others added comments that had not been in it. Max asked no questions this time, but he reached for a piece of paper and occasionally jotted down a few words.

He went on looking at these notes when Peter finally stopped.

Then, looking up, Max said, 'There's an interesting point that you may not be aware of. You didn't mention the first time over that Helen still sees her first husband sometimes.'

'Didn't I?' Peter said. 'Is it important?'

'I don't know. But the fact is, you've made out a pretty good case that Helen's been trying to murder Dan. Did you know that?'

'Because she wants to go back to Marston, d'you mean?'

'No, she could do that without committing murder, if he wanted her, and it doesn't sound much as if he did.'

'Then what's the point?'

'Simply that he's a professor of chemistry and Helen was a student of his. That means she not only knows some chemistry, but knows her way about his laboratory. If she ever meets him there—goes there, perhaps to pick him up for lunch or some such thing—it ought to be very easy indeed for her to lay her hands on some poison.'

'You believe it's true that Dan's being poisoned?'

'Let's assume it for the moment, while we're on the subject of Helen. She's got two possible motives. If Dan died, she'd inherit Grey Gables and she could sell it and move away and live quite differently. I don't know, of course, if she wants to live differently. I hardly know her. What I saw of her I liked. From what you've said of her I gather you've a picture of her as someone who lets anyone who chooses walk all over her. But that may be a pose she's adopted because she's found it's the easiest way to handle Dan. And of course, it may be a role she's got tired of, as she may have got tired of living as if they were poor when an offer from Lingstead's for that barn of a place would make it possible for them to enjoy a few luxuries.'

'What's her other motive?' Peter asked.

'You told me yourself when you described that scene with Juliet. If Helen and Weldon are in love with one another, as Juliet believes, Helen of course would want Dan out of the way. But she may know he wouldn't divorce her, or, if he did, wouldn't provide for her. And Weldon hasn't any money to speak of, has he? According to Kate, who admittedly doesn't like him, he and Juliet live on Dan's generosity a good deal of the time. They may pay a nominal amount towards their keep at Grey Gables, but I think they're very dependent on him. So there's your case against Helen, who, I remember, does most of the cooking down there. So she's got motive, means and opportunity.'

'What about Weldon?' Peter asked. 'Can't you make out a case against him?'

'Yes, certainly, though not quite such a good one. His motive is obvious if he's in love with Helen, or even if he merely knows she's in love with him, so that he can be sure of getting his hands on any money she inherits from Dan. And if he usually carries Dan's tray up to his room, there's his opportunity for adding poison to the food. But I can't tell you anything about how he got hold of the poison. He may have some quite easy access to it that we don't happen to know about. We'd have to leave it to the police to trace it.'

'What's your opinion of what poison it is?'

'I'm not well up in that sort of thing, but doesn't it sound like arsenic? The symptoms have a familiar sound and of course the murderer could speed the job up or slow it down, to simulate a normal illness, as he felt inclined.'

'All right. Whom do we take next?'

'I think I'll take Gina—no, wait a minute!' Max raised a hand to stop Peter interrupting. 'I know you're convinced, for subjective reasons, that the girl couldn't have done it, but let's look at the evidence. It's not inconsiderable as evidence, you know, that Dan himself believes she's guilty. He wrote that, didn't he, to that fellow Rolfe? And she's admitted to you that she hates Dan for having broken up her home.'

'That was just childish exaggeration,' Peter said. 'She doesn't know what hate is.'

'I suspect you exaggerate her childishness,' Max retorted. 'And children know

192

a great deal about hate, even if they don't understand its consequences. Now let me examine the case against her. Like her mother, Gina's got motive, means and opportunity. Motive—that sheer hatred of Dan, with the addition, perhaps, that she likes the idea of her mother inheriting money. Some of it would be very likely to trickle her way. Means—like Helen, she could have got the poison from her father's laboratory. And opportunity—the same as they all have in that house. It must be easy for anyone living there to doctor Dan's food.'

'Suppose then, for argument's sake, it's Gina.' Peter was doing his best to sound as reasonable as Max. 'Why did she go to the trouble of getting me down there? Explain that to me.'

Max lifted his shoulders and let them drop in a shrug that had a touch of mockery in it.

'My dear Peter, you don't seriously expect me to be able to explain everything. I haven't the faintest idea why she wanted you down there. Perhaps she simply likes having you around. But she did go out of her way to impress on you that Dan's illness was something like an ulcer or cancer. You were an unprejudiced witness, so to speak, to her concern for him.'

'That's Gina dealt with then. Now let's take Kate.'

Max grinned. 'You *are* angry with me, aren't you? But you can't seriously expect me to make out a case against my own wife, can you?'

'I'm sure you could if you tried.'

'And you insist I should try. Very well then.' Max brought the tips of his fingers together and contemplated them thoughtfully. 'Opportunity, yes, the same as all the others in the house. Means—as with Weldon, I don't know. She knows an immense number of people and she may have come across someone who'd supply her with arsenic. And if she wanted to kill Dan, she wouldn't be afraid to do it. She's bold, reckless and courageous. But when it comes to motive, I'm defeated. She wouldn't benefit financially by Dan's death. If he's left her as much as his

194

Collected Works, which of course she'd treasure, I'd be surprised. If Helen were the victim and not Dan I might feel a twinge of uneasiness. As I've told you, Kate has to have someone to hero-worship and at the moment it's Dan. But if she's been poisoning him, then it can be only because she's one of those pathological poisoners. You know what I mean. Those people who poison off whole households of people without having a single thing against them and who nurse them tenderly while they're dying. And I've lived a good many years with Kate without noticing any of the symptoms in her.'

'I'm sorry,' Peter said. 'Yes, I was angry at what you said about Gina. Of course Kate can't have done it. Now what about Juliet? She can't have done it either. If the scene she made this afternoon was genuine, and I'm convinced it was, the last thing she'd want is for Helen to be both rich and free.'

Max did not answer for a moment, then he said hesitantly, 'I'm not as certain of that as you are. I can think of two motives for Juliet, both peculiarly ugly.'

'Oh come.'

'Yes indeed. One's quite simple. It's that she expects to have Helen convicted of Dan's murder. As we were saying, the evidence points so plainly at Helen that one begins to wonder if it hasn't been manufactured. And the person most likely to have done that is surely Juliet. The other possibility is a bit more complicated. Suppose Juliet knows she's lost Weldon to Helen and she's resigned herself to the situation, she might then ask herself, what's in it for her? And the answer is, of course, nothing, if Weldon hasn't got any money. But if Helen's got money and she and Weldon take off together, Juliet could probably get a slice of it if she agreed to go ahead with the divorce. So it just might be in her interest to get rid of Dan. And d'you know, the little I know of her, she's always seemed to be an oddly sinister kind of woman. Those dreamy states she gets into and the sort of explosion you saw today add up to something decidedly unbalanced. I can see her as a murderess more easily than any of the others.'

'If I'd said that, you'd have said it was for subjective reasons,' Peter observed.

'I'm afraid that's true. I've no evidence at all that Juliet isn't all loving-kindness.'

'Then there we are, because I don't think we have to analyse Alice Thorpe or the Patons. None of them are close enough to Dan to gain anything by his death. Well, thank you, Max. I'm not sure that this talk has been of any immediate help, but I think, when I've had time to think it over, I'll find it's set some of my thoughts in order.'

'Aren't you forgetting someone?' Max said, looking surprised at Peter's termination of their discussion. 'We haven't dealt with the slightly mysterious Adrian Rolfe.'

'Now that really is absurd,' Peter said. 'He's the one person who couldn't possibly have got at Dan's food. We can leave him out.'

Max looked down at the notes he had made and tapped one gently with his forefinger.

'Suppose he was working with someone else,' he said. 'Someone to whom he supplied the poison. Someone who would benefit by Dan's death. Someone Rolfe's supposed never to have met before, but whom he perhaps knows very well indeed. I'm talking about Gina again, of course, though I suppose it might actually be any of them. But he and Gina may easily be lovers. Perhaps they're even married.'

'Didn't we agree Gina could have got the poison from her father's laboratory?'

'But Rolfe may have some even safer source of supply.'

This time Peter hardly responded. He felt a lethargy which made argument seem simply not worth while. A sense that he had been waiting for Max to say what he had made him wish that he had never started this discussion. Peter could have arrived at this point by himself. Then he could have kept quiet about it, not mentioning it to a soul, least of all to Gina. Now there was no telling what pressure Max might put on him to undertake some wholly repellent course of action.

Max looked thoughtful at the lack of an outburst from Peter, then said, 'We agreed to talk as if we believed that someone's been trying to poison Dan, but there are two things which in my view cast doubts on it.'

Peter swirled the remains of his whisky round in his glass. 'Go on.'

'I'm very ignorant about this sort of thing, mind you,' Max said, 'but it puzzles me how Dan ever came to have the idea that he was being poisoned. Suppose you had all the symptoms Dan had, would you have leapt to the conclusion someone was trying to kill you? Wouldn't you have taken for granted you were suffering from some quite commonplace illness? I think I should myself unless it had been deliberately put into my head that someone was trying to poison me. The second thing is this. Suppose Dan had somehow seriously come to the conclusion that he was being poisoned, how could he have faced eating anything that was given to him in that house? Wouldn't he have felt that anything he ate might have contained the lethal dose that would finish him off? Yet he must have been eating *something*. It may have been very little, only just enough to keep him going, but he hasn't been living on air. And to me that suggests he's never believed in the poison at all.'

'What's the point of the whole charade then?'

'I haven't the least idea.'

'Kate and the others won't listen to the idea that it's for the sake of publicity.'

'I'd be surprised if it was myself. He's a retiring sort of person.'

'Perhaps the easiest thing to believe is that he's had a mental breakdown, dreamt up the bit about being poisoned and is now fleeing from imaginary enemies.'

'I suspect that's the common sense of it,' Max agreed.

'But in that case, do we go to the police or not?'

'It's my impression that you feel you ought to go. So why not do it?'

'It's just that the others on the whole seem against it.'

'Act on your own then.'

'Is that what you'd advise?'

'Good Lord, Peter, I'm not giving you *advice!*' Max protested. 'I've just been hoping I was helping you to clear your own mind up, as you said just now I had. What I'd actually do in your place, I imagine, is wash my hands of the whole business and go home. That's what I was trying to persuade Kate to do just before you telephoned. I've told you I think there's something in the atmosphere down there that's doing her damage. I said to her I thought there was something phoney in the whole situation which I didn't pretend to understand but which I thought she'd be well out of. She wouldn't listen, of course. She takes for granted all the others would go to pieces if she left them and she's very loyal. I don't expect you to listen either—because there's Gina, isn't there? But I'm sure in your place I'd go home.'

Peter got to his feet. 'You wouldn't, you know. You'd be too curious. However, I'll consider it. If there's been no news of Dan when I get back to Sisslebridge, I'll wait till morning, then I'll go to the police and then go home. D'you think that's a sound course of action?'

'As good as any.'

Max stood up too and they both threaded their way through the furniture to the door.

At the front door, holding it open, Max remarked, 'There's one possibility we've carefully avoided discussing and I gather so has everyone else. It's that Dan's dead.'

'Oh, they've talked of his body being found in a ditch, but not very seriously,' Peter said. 'If he is dead and it's from arsenic, someone at Grey Gables must be very anxious to trace him and dispose of the body, because a post-mortem would turn the stuff up very easily.'

'Perhaps he's already been disposed of,' Max replied. 'Perhaps he'd been disposed of even before Weldon found he'd gone missing.'

Peter frowned. 'You're pointing at Rolfe again.'

'He hasn't an alibi.'

'Hell, Max, I've had enough of this!' Peter exclaimed. 'I'm wondering why you haven't made out a case against me.'

'D'you want me to try?'

Peter grinned. 'Perhaps another time. Meanwhile, thanks for bringing your mind to bear on my problem. I'll let you know if there are any interesting developments.'

'Yes, do.'

Peter heard Max's door close quietly behind him as he plunged down the stairs.

He had to walk some distance before he managed to pick up a taxi. The walking did him good. For a little while his mind felt freed from the obsessions that had gripped it for the last twenty-four hours. The rumble of traffic, so familiar to him that he was normally less aware of it than he had been of the silence of Sisslebridge, felt homely to him and helped to draw his thoughts away from the problems that had filled them all day. He found himself thinking of Gina again, not as someone entangled in a sinister web of tragedy, but simply as someone young, fresh and lovely and very important to him.

When presently he rejoined Gina and Rolfe in the restaurant where they had agreed to meet, he found that for the time being they too had managed to forget Dan Braile and were talking about their travels aboard. As soon as Peter had settled himself at their table, they returned to the subject. They were differing about the best way to travel, Gina explaining that she took discomfort in her stride, enjoying the unexpected and liked becoming involved in the lives of strangers, while Rolfe demanded some degree of luxury and was much more interested in ancient monuments than people. Each claimed to be horrorstruck at the attitude of the other, but they were horrorstruck in the friendliest manner and Rolfe's gaze on Gina's bright young face was rapt. Peter felt excluded from the conversation. Neither Gina nor Rolfe had the least interest in how or where he had travelled. He felt some resentment at first, then found it restful. The food was good and he obviously enjoyed it more than either of the others. Which was only proper if you were middle-aged.

If this thought gave him a pang, there was also a relaxing of some tension in it, a tension of which he had not even been aware. All at once it seemed to become unnecessary to make certain efforts, to strain after a variety of things which he was not even sure that he wanted.

But his face must have reflected some of his thoughts, for Gina suddenly turned to him, patted his hand and said, 'Peter, why are you looking so sad?'

He smiled. 'Hadn't you noticed, it's my normal cast of countenance.'

'Yes, I had noticed, as a matter of fact,' she said.

'However, I don't think I've anything special to feel sad about at the moment,' he said, 'except that I feel trapped, like the rest of you, by Dan's behaviour and I don't see when I'm going to get free. What I'd like is to go home and get on with some work. In fact, it's becoming urgent.'

Perhaps he said it to annoy her. She looked at him with a slight frown.

'I think I could tell you where Dan is,' Rolfe remarked, idly crumbling bread beside his plate.

'You could *what?*' Peter felt such an

impulse to shout the question that he countered it by dropping his voice almost to a whisper.

'Oh yes, I think so,' Rolfe replied, nodding his head thoughtfully.

'Where then?'

'If you don't mind, I think I'll check on it before I tell you,' Rolfe said. 'You see, he obviously doesn't want to be found. But if I could talk to him and explain how much worry he's causing and then tell you that he's all right and just wants to be left alone, you wouldn't be caught in that trap any more, would you? You could go home any time you liked.' He paused and added, 'Unless you don't trust me.'

He and Peter exchanged a long, exploratory look.

'I see, you don't,' Rolfe said. 'That's too bad.'

'If you can find Dan, I'd like to talk to him myself,' Peter said.

'All right, when I find him, you shall. *If* I find him. I may be wrong.'

That put an end to the matter for the time being. But somehow it had become impossible to resume their earlier kind of talk. Peter called for the bill and they started back to Sisslebridge.

It was about midnight when Rolfe turned the Jaguar in at the gates of the Manor House Hotel. He had driven Gina up to the door of Grey Gables, where they had heard from Kate, who had come to the door as soon as she heard it opened, that there was still no news of Dan.

She looked more worn and anxious than she had in the morning. Peter told her that he had had a long talk with Max, which he would tell her all about tomorrow, and she nodded listlessly as if she no longer expected her husband to have had anything to contribute. Then Rolfe had driven off.

The door of the hotel was closed but not locked. There was no need to rouse anyone to open it, which was fortunate, because the passageways and stairs were wrapped in their usual silence. Rolfe and Peter said good night to one another and went to their rooms. It had not occurred to Peter before he left for London in the afternoon to turn the knobs on his radiator and the room was dankly cold. The smell of mildew was like a disease. He got into bed as quickly as he could and, after shivering for a few minutes, fell into a light, uneasy sleep.

He had wilder dreams than usual, of the kind that make the night seem filled with stormy activity, yet which vanish completely on waking, leaving behind only a vague sense of terrors endured. When he woke, and what had wakened him he did not know, though he had a feeling that something from outside himself had intruded into his dreams, which had been somehow connected with murder, it was still dark. He put out a hand to switch on the bedside lamp and looked at his watch. To his surprise it was not quite two o'clock. So many events had filled his sleep that he had thought it must be much later. Turning the light off again, he lay back and now found himself lucidly, uncomfortably wakeful.

He wondered how he could have failed to guess before where Dan Braile was. Was it the brandy that he had drunk on the evening of Dan's disappearance that had fogged his mind? He knew the solution to the mystery now. There was really no question about it. There was nowhere else that Dan could have gone on that night of deluge. But at two in the morning what did you do about it? Did you risk waking and perhaps frightening a sick man, or did you wait till morning?

Peter lay on his back for some minutes, staring upward at about the point where the furry patch of mould had erupted from the ceiling. Then he switched the light on again, got up and put on his dressing-gown and slippers. He went out into the passage, felt for a light-switch there and looked to right and left. The second door on his left, he knew, was the door of Rolfe's room. Passing it, Peter went on to the door beyond and edged it softly open.

Pale moonlight fell through uncurtained windows into an empty room. He closed the door and went on to the next one. Emptiness again. He tried a third door and except for a smell of dust and mustiness and disuse, found nothing.

But when he came to the door at the end of the passage, something was different. For one thing, the door was not closed. As he took hold of the handle, it swung inwards. The smell that met him was not the same as that in the other rooms. For a moment he could not think what it was, then it started his heart racing. Wasn't it the smell of a gun that had recently been fired?

The room was pitch dark. The curtains were drawn and no moonlight came in at the windows. Peter groped for the light, could not find it, cursed, fumbled about on the wall, then caught his fingers against the switch and pressed it.

This room had been used. The bed was made and though plainly it had not been slept in, there were dents in it where someone must have been lying down. There was warmth in the room. There were books on the bedside table. There was a crumpled newspaper lying on the floor beside the bed. There was a dark-blue beret on the dressing-table.

There was also a body on the floor.

Adrian Rolfe lay on his side with his knees slightly drawn up and his hands pressed to his breast. Blood had oozed through his fingers, had made a big stain on his green corduroy suit and trickled on to the floor, where it had made a small pool, lurid and glutinous.

CHAPTER IX

After the first moment of recoil Peter went forward. He stooped over Rolfe's body and touched his cheek. Was it imagination that it had already lost the texture of living flesh? It was still quite warm. Peter knew nothing about how long it takes for the chill of death to take possession of limbs, but it could not be very long, he was sure. He touched one of Rolfe's hands. It moved limply under his. There was no stiffening yet. The blood on the floor had hardly started to congeal. So the clap of thunder that had wakened Peter out of his fretful sleep, he thought, had almost certainly been the shot that had killed Rolfe, not more than twenty minutes ago.

Peter looked at his watch again. It was a quarter past two. That was the sort of thing that the police would want to know. Yes, the police. The first thing he had to do was to telephone the police.

There was a telephone, he remembered, in the room behind the bar. Walking backwards until he reached the doorway, as if the dead Rolfe were royal, Peter suddenly turned there and went running down the stairs. He thrust his way through the glass doors that led into the bar to find himself faced with the metal grille which shut off entry to the room behind it.

If there was no other entrance to the room with the telephone, he would have to go to Grey Gables and wake the people there. He felt a deep reluctance to do this. He wanted to talk to the police alone before anyone from that strange house intruded on the scene upstairs. Yet, as he thought of this, it occurred to him that he could not actually be alone in the hotel. The spotty boy at least probably slept on the premises. It might be proper to wake him and tell him to telephone the police himself.

If the boy had been different Peter would probably have followed this course, but the thought of trying to force some understanding of what had happened into that vacant mind sent Peter looking for another entrance to the room behind the bar.

He found one in the kitchen. One of the doors there led into Anna's domain. It was a small room, neatly furnished with a metal desk, a filing cabinet, a typist's chair, one easy chair and a photograph in a heavy walnut frame that stood on the desk.

The photograph was of an elderly couple, opulently dressed in the fashion of the thirties. Anna's parents, for certain. Her likeness to the woman, even allowing for the deformed shoulder, was unmistakable. But if, as they looked, they had been at least sixty when the photograph was taken, they must both be dead by now, whether they had died peacefully in some English suburb or horribly in the gas after sending their daughter to safety. That that daughter would spend her later years as housekeeper in a working men's club in a drab little town like Sisslebridge was something that they could not have expected. The man's well-cut suit, the woman's glossy silk and fine jewellery and the dignity and self-confidence of them both suggested wealth and position. A courageous woman, Anna, to have led her life as she had had to.

Peter, hesitating, reached for the directory, thinking that after all he would telephone Anna before the police. She certainly knew how the room upstairs had been used before the murder had been done there. But he had only just began to turn the pages when he realized that he did not know Anna's surname. Pushing the directory away, he dialled 999.

When he got through to the police station he spoke to a man who identified himself as Sergeant Bolting. He replied to Peter's hurried story of finding a man shot dead in a bedroom in the Manor House Hotel with so little expression in his voice that it might have been thought that shootings in Sisslebridge were commonplace occurrences. But between the brief questions he asked Peter could hear the man's heavy breathing. Peter gave his name, said he had touched nothing on the scene and would see that no one else

215

did, supposing he could find anyone at all in the place, and that he would wait there for the police to arrive. Then, as the sergeant rang off, he went looking for the spotty boy.

Instead of finding him, he blundered into the bedroom of the stout woman whom he had seen in the kitchen that morning, talking to Anna. She lay on her back in bed, gently snoring, with her hair in rollers and her plump bare arms flung out on either side of the soft hummocks of her body. When Peter switched on the light she gave a little yelp of fright, then woke fully and gave him a round-eyed stare of incredulity.

Clutching her bedclothes up to her neck, she said, 'Haven't you come into the wrong room, dear?'

Peter was in too single-minded a state to notice the beginnings of a leer on her face.

'I beg your pardon, Mrs...?'

'Pierce,' she said.

'I beg your pardon, Mrs Pierce, I was looking for that boy who seems to run the show here, but I'm glad I've found you. The police will be arriving in a short time and I'm sure you'd like to be ready for them. Perhaps you could get that boy up too. They'll want to question him.'

'Arthur?' she said.

'Arthur, is it? Well yes, I'm sure they'll want to talk to you and Arthur.'

She began to look angry. 'Here, what *is* this? What've you called the police for at this time of night? If it's something you've missed, let me tell you, Arthur's as honest as the day. And no one's ever had a word to say against me in my life...' She paused. She began to look scared. 'I suppose it's something to do with—with *him.*'

'I think it probably is,' Peter answered.

'But we done nothing wrong, only let him stay here quietly. There's nothing wrong in that. Anyone can stay here, it's a hotel, and if they say, "Don't mention I'm here, I want a little peace and quiet, so keep it to yourselves," what's wrong with that?'

'Nothing, only one of your other visitors went into the room Mr Braile's been using and got himself shot dead. That's why I sent for the police.'

Her eyes grew round again with staring disbelief. 'Shot dead? Who?'

'Mr Rolfe.'

'Ah, that one,' she said and nodded, as if she found this easier to understand than the other things that Peter had said. 'I thought he was up to no good. The moment I seen him I didn't trust him. Too smooth for me. And those clothes. You're up to no good, I said to myself, and I've a way of being right about things like that.'

'Only it was Mr Rolfe who got killed,' Peter said. 'I'd say it was someone else who was up to no good.'

'Well, what was he doing in that room there in the middle of the night? Come to think of it, what were you? How do I know you didn't shoot him yourself? How do I know you aren't a murderer?'

Growing horror had appeared on her face as she followed her own line of thought. She looked as if she had nearly achieved a state when she would see fit to start screaming.

'I'm sure the police will look into that possibility,' Peter said soothingly. 'Meanwhile, if I were you, I'd get dressed and get Arthur up too. I don't think there'll be much sleep for us for the rest of the night. And can you tell me if Anna has a telephone?'

'Anna? You want her to come here in the middle of the night?' she protested. 'She lives at Burley's End. That's all of two miles away, and it's a lonely road and you say yourself there's a murderer loose.'

'I only want to talk to her,' Peter said. 'Has she a telephone?'

'Yes, Sisslebridge 336.'

'Thank you.'

Peter closed the door behind him and went downstairs.

He went into the little room behind the bar and dialled Anna's number. The telephone rang on and on without an answer, but he went on holding it to his ear, thinking that it must wake her sooner or later.

At last her sleepy voice croaked at him, 'Yes?'

'Anna, this is Peter Harkness,' he said. 'I want to talk to Mr Braile. He's with you, isn't he?'

'I do not understand you,' Anna replied. 'You ring me up in the middle of the night and you ask me something like that. I do not understand.'

'He's been staying here, hasn't he?' Peter said. 'You needn't pretend he hasn't. I've been talking to Mrs Pierce. He's been staying here and he left some time today. And there's a dead man in his room now, Adrian Rolfe, who came here to see him. Rolfe's been shot, I think. I've sent for the police. If Braile's with you, hadn't you better let me talk to him?'

'I do not understand,' Anna said mulishly. 'Why should you think he is here?'

'Because you've been looking after him. You're his friend. He turned to you for help when he left his house the other evening. I think you're probably looking after him still.'

'You are wrong, Mr Harkness.'

'Then where is he? I'm sure you know.'

'You are wrong.'

'I don't think I believe you.'

'I tell you, I know nothing.'

'Well, I'll tell the police all I know, so they'll probably be along to see you later.'

'Mr Harkness, Mr Braile has never harmed anyone in his life. He has a good heart. He has very fine feelings. I do not understand about the man Rolfe, but Mr Braile had nothing to do with it.'

'I haven't suggested he had. All the same, wherever he is, I'd get in touch with him and tell him what's happened.'

Peter rang off.

Strolling out into the passage and along it to the front door, he wondered how long it would take the police to arrive. Opening the door, he stepped out into the night. The sky was clear and the stars were brilliant. By their light he could see, dotted here and there in the lawns surrounding the building, pale clumps of daffodils that had managed to raise their heads again after the battering that they had had from the rain. He also saw that a surprising number of lights were still on in Grey Gables. Someone had stayed up late. Watching for Dan, perhaps.

But it was cold in the garden, so Peter turned back into the hotel. He was closing the door behind him when it occurred to him that it had not been locked when he went out. Neither had it been locked when he and Rolfe had returned from London, although there had been no one about. A murderer could have come and gone without any difficulty.

Only a few minutes later a car turned into the drive. It had two constables in it, big, fresh-faced young men with the local burr in their voices. They asked to be taken straight up to the room where the dead man lay. One of them came out almost immediately, not looking quite as fresh-faced as before. He asked who else there was in the house besides Peter, who replied that so far as he knew there was no one but the cook, Mrs Pierce, and a boy called Arthur, neither of whom had appeared yet. But as another police car stopped in the drive Mrs Pierce came down the stairs and went to answer the door. She had waited to dress herself in a black jersey dress and to take the rollers out of her hair and brush it out in stiff curls around her face. Pink, fur-edged bedroom slippers were the only sign of informality that she had allowed herself.

'I'm Mrs Pierce,' she greeted the first man who came in at the door. 'I'm in charge, you could say, but I don't know anything, only what Mr Harkness told me. We ought to phone Mr Danby, that's what I think, only he's in Spain and I don't know his number and I don't even know what time of day it is there.'

She spoke as if Spain were at the other side of the world.

The man she was addressing introduced himself as Detective-Superintendent Crab-tree and the man who followed him as Sergeant Woodbury. The superintendent was a slender but well-built man who surprised Peter by appearing no older than he was himself. Somewhere tucked away at the back of Peter's mind was a feeling that a fairly senior policeman should be some sort of a father figure. Peter had long ago passed the stage when it had surprised him to notice that constables controlling traffic were mere boys, but he still had a feeling that a man capable of taking charge on an occasion such as this should obviously have an experience of life that Peter himself had not yet achieved.

Not that this might not be the case with Superintendent Crabtree, even if he was actually a year or two younger than Peter. He had a narrow, strong-boned face with shrewd, curiously unblinking light-blue eyes, close-cropped dark hair, a deep, quiet voice and he moved with lightness, yet with deliberation, which helped to give him an air of authority which would make him an excellent father figure in ten years' time.

For the present Peter could imagine it being irritating on some occasions, though just now it seemed on the whole reassuring. It absolved him of responsibility. He went into the bar, switched on the electric fire, sat down near it and prepared to wait for whatever should happen next.

Driven by similar feelings, no doubt, Mrs Pierce soon appeared and sat down facing him on the other side of the fire. She sat with her hands tightly folded and her lips pressed together. It looked as if she were letting steam work up inside her which she would presently eject at the policemen. A few minutes later they were joined by Arthur. The boy was dressed in dark trousers and his not very clean white jacket and was carrying a key with which he unlocked the grille that closed off the bar and without asking questions poured out a stiff whisky for Peter, a rum and lemon for Mrs Pierce and a ginger ale for himself. It was the first time that Peter realized that the boy might not be subnormal.

It sounded as if more and more men were arriving at the hotel. Heavy feet tramped up and down the stairs and voices called out orders. The place had not sounded so inhabited since the meeting of the Sisslebridge Arts League. Which was only yesterday evening. Or, to be more accurate, since this was already early morning, two evenings ago. It hardly seemed possible. To Peter's mind a great gulf yawned between this time, when he was sitting in his dressing-gown in the little bar, waiting and wondering what new demand was to be made upon him, and the time when Gina's telephone call to his flat had made him decide to come here to find out why she needed him.

The new demand, when it came, was made by Superintendent Crabtree, who appeared in the doorway and said, 'Mr Harkness, if I could have a few words with you.'

Peter got up and followed him out. The superintendent had chosen Anna's little office as the most comfortable place for conducting his enquiries. A constable with an open notebook was waiting there. Crabtree settled himself at the desk, as if in doing so he were taking possession of the room, and gestured to Peter to make himself comfortable in the one armchair.

'I understand it was you who discovered the body, Mr Harkness,' Crabtree said. 'It was you who telephoned us, wasn't it?'

'Yes,' Peter said.

'But I don't understand what took you into that room at that time of night,' Crabtree went on. 'Can you explain it?'

'Quite simply,' Peter answered. 'A noise woke me up. I thought...' He paused. 'No, it isn't simple. I don't know why I said it was. It's very complicated.'

'Suppose we begin with this noise then,' Crabtree said. 'What kind of noise was it?'

'I don't know. Something woke me suddenly, but I didn't think much about it at the time because I immediately started to think, as it seemed to me very lucidly, and a number of things that had been confused in my mind became quite clear. So I got up and went hunting from room to room... Not for Rolfe, of course. I thought he was in his room, Number 18, and I avoided that deliberately and went looking into all the other rooms and I found him in Number 22, shot dead. So I assume it was the noise of the shot that wakened me, because of the smell of the shot in the room and the obvious fact that he hadn't been dead long.'

'Did you hear anything else after you woke up?' Crabtree asked. 'Footsteps? A car driving away?'

'No, nothing.'

'Can you tell me at all what you started thinking about when you woke up?' Crabtree went on. 'It seems to be relevant.'

'It certainly is, but to explain the whole thing...' Peter rested his head on a hand, wondering where to begin. 'Perhaps you know Daniel Braile,' he said.

'I know of him,' Crabtree said. 'I've never met him.'

'You know he lives over there at Grey Gables?'

'Yes.'

'Well, the evening before last he disappeared. He'd been ill, on and off, for two or three weeks. There was disagreement about what was the matter with him. There are a number of people staying in the house at the moment. They all seem to have begun by thinking it was food poisoning. Then he got better, then it started all over again, and that time they decided it was gastric 'flu. There were some attempts to get him to see a doctor, but he wouldn't have one. And he got worse and it became obvious he wasn't going to be able to take part in a sort of literary chat they were going to hold here that evening—the evening before last. So I was asked by Mrs Rowley, who's one of the guests and an old friend of mine, to come down and take his place. And I came and all the household except Mr Braile came over for the affair—'

'One moment,' Crabtree interrupted. 'They all came, leaving this sick man by himself?'

'Well, no,' Peter said. 'I shouldn't have said that. An old lady, Miss Thorpe, stayed behind with him in case he should want anything, but she fell asleep by the fire so no one knows exactly what happened in the house while the rest of them were gone. Mr Weldon was the first to go back. He'd been worrying from the first about leaving Mr Braile virtually alone and he went back on his own before the party broke up and he found Braile had vanished. He'd apparently got up by himself, got dressed, put on a waterproof, gum-boots and a beret, taken an umbrella and walked out into the night. You remember how it rained that evening. They were all flabbergasted because they thought he was much too ill to do anything like that, and two young people, the Patons, who are staying there, went out to search for him in the grounds in case he'd gone out and collapsed somewhere. But they didn't find him and Weldon stayed up all night in case Braile should come wandering in, perhaps not even knowing what he'd been doing. But he didn't. And today—yesterday—they all began arguing whether or not to call the police.'

'Why didn't they?' Crabtree asked.

'Well, the evidence was, wasn't it, that Braile had gone away by himself?' Peter said. 'It looked as if he was a good deal stronger than any of them had realized and that he'd simply wanted to get away by himself for a while.'

'Yes, I see.'

'And if that was how it was, he wasn't going to be pleased if we sent the police looking for him. But we thought we'd check up on whether or not he'd gone to a flat he has in London and three of us, Rolfe and Braile's stepdaughter, Miss Marston, and I drove up this afternoon to see if he'd turned up there. But he hadn't, so we had dinner in town and came back. We delivered Miss Marston at Grey Gables and Rolfe and I came back here and went to bed. And I went to sleep and then this noise I was talking about wakened me and I realized at once—in fact, I couldn't think how I hadn't thought of it before—that Braile must have been in this hotel all the time.'

'So you went looking for him.'

'Yes.'

'And that's how you found Rolfe's body at two in the morning in the room that Braile had been occupying.'

'Yes.'

The detective nodded. His unblinking blue stare had been on Peter's tired face all the time that he had been talking.

'Mr Harkness, you've left several things out,' he said. 'For instance, what made you suddenly so certain that Daniel Braile was in this hotel?'

'He could hardly have been anywhere else,' Peter answered. 'First, he was a sick man, very weak. I'd heard that from several people. So wherever he'd gone, it couldn't have been far. And the road in one direction was flooded and in the other there are no houses for about two miles. And this hotel seems to stand open, night and day, and there's no one at any reception desk to see who comes in and out. In fact, I believe you could stay here for days on end without anyone discovering you existed. There's hardly any staff at all because the place is closing down in a few days. And of course Braile had a friend here whom he could count on to help him if he wanted to go into hiding, the barmaid, Anna. I don't know her other name.'

'Weinstock,' Crabtree said.

'Oh, you know her.'

'Yes, she's worked in these parts, mostly

in hotels, ever since she came over as a refugee in the thirties. At first, of course, until she got her naturalization, she had to keep reporting to us. That was before my time, but some of the older chaps know her quite well.'

'Well, she's a pretty close friend of Braile's, as she tells it,' Peter said. 'I think she'd do anything for him. So if he managed to stagger over as far as this and got hold of her while the meeting was on in the dining-room, I'm sure she'd have taken him straight upstairs and put him to bed there and kept him hidden for as long as he wanted. Then there was the bacon she was frying in the morning...' Peter checked himself, feeling that what he had been about to say would sound absurd.

'Yes?' Crabtree said with interest.

'It's just that when Rolfe and I came down for breakfast yesterday morning,' Peter went on, 'there was no one around, so we went to the kitchen hopefully looking for someone and there was Anna at the stove, frying bacon. And she said she'd bring some breakfast to us in a few minutes. But she didn't. It was at least a quarter of an hour before anyone started taking any notice of us and longer still before any food arrived. So I think the bacon she was frying when we found her must have been for someone else. That's a ridiculously small point and I may be quite mistaken, but when I woke up this morning I felt it was absolutely obvious she'd been cooking breakfast for Braile. Then there was whatever she was cooking at lunch-time. It smelt very good and she said it was for the staff and that she could only give us sandwiches, but again, whatever it was, I think it was for Braile.'

Crabtree smiled. 'And you think he's with Anna Weinstock now.'

'I thought so,' Peter said. 'Before you got here I telephoned her, saying I wanted to speak to him. She denied that he was there, but I don't believe her. I think while Rolfe and I were away in London yesterday afternoon she got him out of the place to her own home. Mrs Pierce and Arthur may be able to tell you something about how it was managed.'

'So you don't think he murdered Rolfe?'

Peter looked at him blankly. 'Why ever should he?'

'Why should anyone? We know next to nothing about Rolfe, except for his home address. We found that in his wallet. What can you tell us about him, Mr Harkness?'

'Only what he told us himself,' Peter said. 'He said he wrote Braile a fan-letter out of the blue, that Braile replied and that they started corresponding. Then Braile pressed Rolfe to come down here for a visit and eventually Rolfe came, arriving just after Braile's disappearance had been discovered. But Rolfe wasn't expected by anyone in the household. Braile hadn't said anything about having invited him. So he came over here to stay the night and then stayed on—'

'And was killed. If you don't think Braile shot him, what do you think of the idea that someone shot him, thinking he was Braile? After all, someone else could have worked it out, just as you did, where Braile was hiding.'

'That strikes me as rather more probable.'

'Mr Harkness—' The smile that had lingered on Crabtree's face broadened into a sardonic grin. 'You don't think it isn't obvious that you're still leaving something out, do you? Must I dig for it? Won't you make it easy for me?'

Peter leant back in his chair. He withdrew his gaze from the other man's and gazed up at the ceiling. If he had had more sleep, he thought, he would not have blundered into the position in which he now was. It would after all have been far more intelligent to tell the whole truth from the start than to be caught out.

'Well, yes,' he admitted, 'there's the little matter that Braile thought he was being poisoned. It's what he was running away from.'

Crabtree nodded. 'Yes, as you told it, Braile had to be running away from something and you gave the impression of knowing what it was.'

'I didn't, of course,' Peter said. 'I haven't talked to Braile myself. It's only what I've been told by some of the others.'

'By Rolfe, for one,' Crabtree said. 'He had a letter from Braile in his wallet. But the letter didn't invite Rolfe to come down here. It told Rolfe that Braile suspected he was being poisoned and that the probable poisoner was his stepdaughter, Gina Marston.'

Peter's face flamed red. He started to say something, clamped his jaws shut and sat scowling down at his clasped hands.

'Now tell me what you know about this poison,' Crabtree said. There was amusement in his deep, soft voice which made Peter furious with himself for having been taken so by surprise and, even more, for showing it.

'Nothing,' Peter said. 'Only what the others have been saying, and I haven't believed half of it. But Gina Marston was the one person who took Braile's illness seriously. She was afraid it was cancer. She wanted him to see a doctor. She got me down here to help her persuade him that he ought to see a doctor.'

The door opened and a constable looked in.

'Mr Braile and Miss Weinstock are here, sir,' he said. 'They want to talk to you.'

CHAPTER X

Superintendent Crabtree got up quickly and went into the passage.

Peter, taking this as dismissal, followed him out.

In the pink-carpeted hallway, under the dim light that hung from the dusty, ornate ceiling, Daniel Braile was standing, one hand on an umbrella which he had evidently been using as a walking-stick, and the other on Anna Weinstock's shoulder.

She was wearing slacks and a sheepskin jacket. A woollen scarf was knotted over her dark hair. Her small pinched face was pale and apprehensive.

Daniel Braile was also very pale. He looked almost too fragile to stand. His flesh, only just enough to cover his bones, had an illusory appearance of transparency. His eyes were sunken into his head. But there was no dullness about them, for the anger in them made them brilliant. He was in corduroy trousers, a cream-coloured Aran sweater and gum-boots.

He drew a deep breath as if it were difficult for him to speak. Then he said in a weak but pleasant voice, 'Good evening, Mr Crabtree. We've never met, but of course I've heard of you. Miss Weinstock gave me the message about poor Rolfe and I persuaded her it was my duty to come back. I've been staying here, of course, since I left my home, until this afternoon when she allowed me to move into her cottage at Burley's End. A neighbour drove us over. I'm shocked beyond words at this news about Rolfe. If I can help in any way, please tell me how.'

The breath whistled out of him as he finished. His attention appeared to have been so exclusively on the effort of speaking steadily that he had seemed not to be aware of Peter, standing behind Crabtree, or else, in the state of extreme weakness that he certainly was in, did not recognize him.

Crabtree reached out, slipping an arm

under Braile's, relieving Anna of the weight on her shoulder.

'I'm sure you can help us, Mr Braile,' Crabtree said. 'But I think we should go upstairs so that you can lie down. It doesn't look to me as if you should be up and about.'

'No, no, I'm quite well, I'm very well,' Braile answered. 'Much better than I was. Anna is a splendid nurse. Her office, if that's what you've been using, will suit me perfectly. Anna will wait for me and take me home again presently. As soon as possible. To her home, I mean, not mine. Her little house is so peaceful. It's wonderful to feel such peace. There's more healing in it than in all the drugs in the world.'

Though he spoke of peace, the dark fire in his eyes burned as fiercely as ever.

'I'd like to ask Miss Weinstock a few questions before you leave,' Crabtree said.

'Yes, yes,' Anna said. 'I tell you all I can. But please be careful of Mr Braile. He is a very sick man.'

Crabtree nodded and led Braile gently

241

into the little office, shutting the door behind them.

Anna let her hands fall to her sides, as if, now that Braile did not need them to support him, she had no further use for them. She gave Peter a grave look.

'I'm sorry I lied to you when you telephoned,' she said. 'He was there in my house, of course, but he'd gone to bed and I was afraid of what the shock of hearing about Mr Rolfe might do to him. But when I woke him he made me tell him what you said and then he made me bring him here. He is such an honourable, conscientious man. I have a very kind neighbour who helped me with him. He is still terribly ill.'

'Is it true that he's any better?' Peter asked, wondering how much life that skeleton of a man had left in him.

She nodded vigorously. 'Oh yes, he is eating more and he is not so weak. I am not giving him too much food all at once, it would only upset him, but I am giving him a little whenever he feels he can take it. It would be best if he would go to hospital but he refuses. So he is staying with me. It is very simple, my cottage, but I can make him comfortable. And soon, tomorrow, perhaps, we know the truth about his condition, then we can think what we should do. Now I make coffee for us all, no? You would like some coffee, isn't it?'

'Very much,' Peter said, thinking that while she was making the coffee he would get dressed.

While he was dressing and giving his chin a hurried scrape with his razor, he glanced out of the window and noticed that the lights in Grey Gables had all gone out. So they had given Dan up for the time being. It was a little strange that no one appeared to have heard the police cars arriving, or if they had heard them, had not been stirred by curiosity to find out what was happening. Perhaps they were all too tired after the watching and waiting. He went downstairs again, passing a policeman and a man with a camera coming up, and saw Anna carrying a tray ahead of him into the bar. Arthur, still in one of the chairs there, had fallen asleep.

Anna gave a sigh when she saw him.

'Poor Arthur, he is a good boy,' she said. 'He helped me this afternoon with Mr Braile while you and Mr Rolfe were in London. But how lucky he is to be able to sleep so. How lucky to be so young. I have not slept now for two nights. Sometimes I go two, three nights without sleeping. Then I become sorry for myself and remember the past and fear the future. But Arthur, I think, has no past or future to fear and never will have. How fortunate he is.'

'You don't really think so.' Peter took the cup of coffee that she had poured for him. 'Nobody really wants to be a cabbage. Probably even Arthur has secret hopes and ambitions that inspire him now and then.'

'More likely they make him miserable.' She poured out coffee for herself. 'I once had the hope to sing in the opera in Vienna. It never would have happened because of my ugly shoulder, but I did not understand that and I had begun to study. My life was all joy. Oh, such joy! But to remember joy can be a great sorrow. I would very happily be a cabbage. A cabbage without knowing it, that would be best of all.'

'Yesterday you said how glad you were that you were going to be housekeeper here when the place becomes a club,' Peter reminded her. 'You said there would be plenty of life then and that that would be good.'

'I said that?' she said vaguely as if she were not sure that she remembered it. 'But perhaps I do not stay. I must think. Perhaps not.'

She gave a rather secretive little smile. Peter looked at her curiously.

'Have you got something else in mind?'

'Ach, I have my dreams, like everybody else. Perhaps it is only dreams. I think I become housekeeper here, as I told you. But now tell me about this Mr Rolfe. I still know nothing and I do not understand what is happening. How can he be dead?'

As briefly as he could, having grown a little tired of the subject, Peter told her why he had gone prowling from room to room in the hotel in the middle of the night and how he had found Rolfe's body.

The coffee was very good. He drank it quickly and held his cup out to be filled again. He was aware that there was something that he wanted to ask Anna, yet for the moment he could not remember what it was. She nodded from time to time as he spoke, muttered something to herself in German as if her feelings went too deep for her limited English, and as he finished sat shaking her head broodingly.

'He was young too, very young,' she said. 'He must have interfered in something dangerous. What other reason could there be to kill him? Have you thought, Mr Harkness, perhaps if he had not been killed going into that room in the night, you might have been killed instead when you went in?'

She did not sound particularly shocked at the idea, only interested.

'I'm not sure that I understand you,' he said.

'I do not understand either,' she replied. 'I speak what comes into my head. But there was someone in there, waiting for someone, no? But there are some things we shall know soon, that is sure.'

It reminded Peter of what it was that he wanted to ask her.

'Anna, you said a little while ago that we should soon know the truth about Mr Braile's condition and that then you could think out what to do. What did you mean?'

'Just what I said,' she answered. 'The truth about his illness.'

'Then he's agreed to see a doctor after all?'

'No, no, he says no doctor must know for the present. But when he came here first we put some specimens—you understand me—in bottles and yesterday morning I posted them to a cousin of mine who is a chemist and works in a laboratory and I telephoned him to say it must all be in the utmost confidence but it was necessary for me to know if there was poison in what I sent. Arsenic, I said. Mr Braile believes it is arsenic. And my cousin said the test for this is easy and quickly done, so, as I said, we shall soon know if Mr Braile is right and those people there have been poisoning him, or if he has some true disease that perhaps is killing him. I think my cousin will telephone later today. Then Mr Braile can think what he will do.'

'To which of them, I wonder,' Peter said.

'He knows.'

'Will he be telling the police all this?' he said.

'I think so. Because he has told me to tell the police everything I know. He does not ask it of me to tell lies.'

'You'll enjoy telling all you can, won't you?'

She gave Peter a startled stare, then she turned her hands up as if to show that they were empty, that she carried no weapons.

'You may be right,' she said with a sad sound of confession in her voice. 'I am so angry. You don't know how angry I am. That anyone could do such a thing to him, to such a man. I would do murder myself in revenge if I knew who it was. Perhaps that is evil.'

'Then he hasn't told you who it is?'

'No, but it's one of them over there, that's all I know. It must be one of them.'

'You've made up your mind, before hearing from your cousin, that Mr Braile's been poisoned?'

'No, I only hope so.'

'You *hope*...?'

'Of course. If it was arsenic and he stays with me and eats good food, he will soon recover. But if that was illusion, then...' She paused and shook her head. 'Then I think he will soon die,' she added desolately.

She closed her eyes. Peter did not think that it was from drowsiness but that she was withdrawing from him and his questions into a private world of grief and fear.

Leaning back, closing his own eyes, he gave himself up for a little while to an immense weariness. It was a weariness compounded of shock, bewilderment and anxiety. The discovery of a dead body was certainly a very exhausting thing. He drifted into the half-sleep of nervous stress and was only wakened from it by hearing Dan Braile speaking.

'I don't understand how you got involved in this, Peter,' he was saying. 'How did it happen?'

Peter sat up with a start. Anna had gone. Arthur had gone too. Braile was sitting in the chair that Anna had occupied, nursing a cup of coffee. He looked relaxed and peaceful as if talking at length to the police had done him good.

'Kate wanted me to come down to take your place in that Arts League affair,' Peter answered.

'Ah yes, I'd forgotten about that.' A slight frown creased Dan's high, narrow forehead. 'I've been under a strain recently, you know. I dare say I've forgotten a lot of things. Kate, was it?'

'Yes, and Gina.' Peter watched to see if the mention of her name had any noticeable effect on Dan.

Except that his small, solemn mouth

puckered in a dubious way, he showed nothing.

'Gina—she's a friend of yours, isn't she?' he said. 'I ought to thank you for standing in for me. Not only because it saved me from letting all those good people down, but because it made my escape from that terrible house possible. They've all been watching me, you know, hardly ever leaving me alone. It's made things very difficult.'

'*All* of them?' Peter said.

Dan pushed his fingers through his hair. His face was moist with nervous sweat. Coming here tonight from Anna's cottage at Burley's End must have been a great strain for him.

'How could I tell which of them to trust?' he asked. 'The ones who weren't guilty would have tried to restrain me as much as the one who was. They were afraid I was mad, you see. I'd told them, I'd warned them that I believed I was being poisoned. I thought that would scare whoever it was and put a stop to it. But it made no difference. I had another attack of

251

sickness, far worse than before, only a day or two later. Alice Thorpe saved my life.'

'Alice Thorpe?' Peter said incredulously. 'The old lady?'

'Yes, yes, a wonderful woman, intelligent, courageous. A rare personality. I've always admired her. Her talent is small, of course. She's only published two books of verse, both of them when she was quite young, but the work is good. Sensitive, honest. When the source dried up, she didn't pretend it hadn't.'

'No doubt she had an independent income,' Peter observed drily.

'As a matter of fact, no,' Dan replied. 'She was a social worker, dealing with the mentally handicapped, until she had to retire. She was devoted to her work. Now she has a small pension, that's all, and of course the old age pension. That's why I was particularly glad to have her to stay at Grey Gables. It gave her the kind of change that she probably couldn't have afforded otherwise.'

Peter regretted his sneer.

'How did she save you?' he asked. 'By

helping you to get away?'

'Yes, that. I managed to walk over here alone, but she told me when everyone had gone and helped me to get dressed.'

'So she wasn't really asleep when Weldon found her.'

'She may have been, after the effort she'd made. But she really saved me by telling me that she had overheard two of them talking about the poison in the kitchen. Kate and Gina. They were discussing, apparently when to start stepping up the dose. They didn't realize that she could hear them. The old are often mistaken for deaf when all that's wrong with them is that they're a little slow. Because they react slowly to what is said to them, people repeat it, raise their voices, shout at them and confuse them further. Alice's hearing is excellent if nothing distracts her.'

'Just a minute,' Peter said. 'You're confusing me now. You said Kate and Gina?'

'Yes, it's strange, isn't it? I mean that Kate should be involved. I don't pretend to understand it. But Alice definitely said Kate.'

Peter shook his head. 'There's something wrong about that somewhere. We'll talk about Gina in a moment, but talking of Kate, what possible motive could she have for wanting you dead?'

'That's what I've kept asking myself,' Dan said. 'And I can think of only one answer. Envy.'

Peter looked at Dan to see how serious he was. But Dan nearly always looked serious. Even when he laughed his eyes hardly ever lit up. They were bright enough now, but it was still with that smouldering anger.

'Do you mean she might have wanted you to die because she knows you're a better writer than she is?' Peter asked.

'Stranger things have happened.'

'I don't believe it. I wonder—do you know if Miss Thorpe *saw* Kate and Gina talking in the kitchen, or did she only overhear them? I mean, could she have been mistaken about whose voices she heard? Gina, for instance, has a voice very like Helen's. They've no physical resemblance, but their voices are very alike.'

'To tell the truth, I'm not sure how much Miss Thorpe saw,' Dan said. 'It didn't occur to me to ask her. She was so sure herself about whom she'd heard. And after she'd told me about it—I was already suspicious about my illness, you know, it didn't seem to me natural, that's why I wouldn't have a doctor—she used to smuggle food up to me at night. That's what kept me going. I was scared to eat anything that came up to me on my tray, so I used to mess it about a bit to make it look as if I'd eaten something, but in fact I subsisted for days on what she managed to bring me. It couldn't be much, of course, or they'd have noticed that food was missing from the refrigerator, but I've never needed much food and I really managed very well.'

'What I don't understand,' Peter said, 'is why your suspicion that your illness wasn't what you call natural should have made you refuse to have a doctor.'

'But that's obvious,' Dan answered. 'If I was being poisoned then it was essential for the poisoner that I should see a doctor. A not very competent doctor who'd prescribe antibiotics for a non-existent infection and happily sign my death certificate when I died. As long as I absolutely refused to see a doctor I reasoned that I was relatively safe, because if I died without seeing one there'd have to be a post-mortem and the poison would be discovered.'

Peter drew a long breath. 'So that's why you suspected Gina!'

'Of course.'

'You thought that just because she was the one who tried hardest to get you to see a doctor, she was probably your murderer.'

'Naturally. Not forgetting that conversation overheard by Alice Thorpe.'

'But the other was the reason for your accusation against her in the letter you wrote to Rolfe.'

'Ah, that letter. If only I'd never written it.'

Dan let his head droop forward on his

chest and his hands hang loosely between his knees. They were long hands with slender fingers. Not very strong hands, but expressive. The slight curling of the fingers made them look as if he itched to claw with them at the throat of someone he could have named if he had chosen.

'If I'd never written,' he went on, 'the poor young fellow would never have come down and he'd still be alive. I feel a terrible sense of responsibility. But I don't know if you know what it's like to be in a houseful of people, none of whom you dare entirely trust, even your own wife, and you're ill and helpless. There was a fearful loneliness in it, something I can't describe. Loneliness—oh, God, I've always thought of myself as rather enjoying it, even needing it, you know, to make those voyages of discovery into my own nature that a writer needs. But now I realize I've never known what it meant. All I wanted was the pleasantness of being quietly alone, not that awful sense of being encircled by people any one of whom might be my direst enemy. Looking at the faces, trying to guess who it was, how many of them were in it...I actually felt a kind of relief when I realized it was Gina.'

'The one person you should have trusted.'

'Trusted?' Dan's soft voice rose sharply. 'My dear Peter, have you ever looked into that girl's eyes?'

'Often.'

'And what do you see? The blank, inhuman stare of an animal. She's dangerous, very dangerous.'

'I don't think so.'

'Are you in love with her?'

'I... Well, I'm not sure.'

'Gina,' Dan said quietly, almost to himself. 'You know she's never made any secret of the fact that she hates me.'

'I think it's a child's sort of hate, which is three-quarters play.'

Dan gave a weary shake of his head. 'Gina stopped playing a long time ago. Perhaps when I took her mother away from her father. The girl grew up then all of a sudden and very painfully. If I'd understood what it would do to her perhaps

I'd have left Helen and gone away—though it's probably gross self-deception to think I could have been so unselfish. I was desperately in love with Helen. Her quiet and her gentleness. The wonderful sense of strength and power that it gave me. I'd never experienced anything like it before. Of course it didn't last.'

'Why "of course"?' Peter asked, wanting to keep Dan talking because sooner or later he might say something that would seem important. At the same time Peter felt that it was wrong to let the man go on, because he was too ill and exhausted to know what he was saying.

'Because she's ready to give the same kind of feeling to anybody,' Dan said. 'So it loses it value. One even gets tired of it. Marston had got tired of it before I ever came on the scene. He'd already started an affair with that woman he married later, and I saw myself as rescuing Helen from humiliation and loss. Naturally Gina doesn't know that. Perhaps we ought to have told her, but she was only thirteen and nowadays we don't talk about that time much. But I've tried everything I could to win that girl's affection. You just don't know how I've tried. And it was all quite useless. I was the destroyer who'd put an end to her happy childhood. No, Peter, for your own sake, don't think of Gina as a child. She's old—old and twisted—far beyond her years.'

Peter was silent. What Dan had said gave him the feeling that he had only half-understood the man before. At the same time he wanted fiercely to defend Gina. But Dan looked too weak and vulnerable to attack.

After a moment Peter said, 'Once you knew who wanted you to call a doctor, why didn't you call one? That couldn't have done any harm.'

Dan made an unexpected sound that might have been a chuckle.

'If you knew our doctors! There's Barrow, whom you probably met the other evening. A delightful fellow, but all he ever thinks about is acting. He never wanted to be a doctor, but his father had been one and his father before him and no one in the family would believe that you could make a livelihood on the stage. So they dragooned young Barrow into medicine, which he's always hated, and which he managed to forget most of as soon as he'd learnt it. If he's prodding your middle to find out where it hurts he doesn't listen to what you tell him but probably asks if you ever saw Peter Finch as Iago. And Dr Gains, one of his partners, is an advanced alcoholic. I like him, he's a very warm-hearted, serious sort of man and he's not a bad doctor when he's sober, but lethal when he isn't and that's most of the time. The only one in the partnership who's reliable is Dr Morrison and she's in hospital just now, having a baby. As a matter of fact, I've wondered if the time for my murder was chosen to coincide with the time Dr Morrison was going to be laid up.' He made the chuckling sound again. 'Too far-fetched? You don't think it's likely? I'll tell you something, I know I've lost all sense of reality lately. Everything that's been happening to me ever since Lingstead's offered me that hundred and sixty thousand has been so extraordinary that I've stopped being able to assess what's genuinely probable and what's a sick fantasy.'

'A hundred and sixty thousand!' Peter exclaimed. 'All that for Grey Gables?'

'That shakes you, doesn't it?' Dan said, looking up at him with a rather puckish smile. 'You always shake people if you talk of large sums of money. Lingstead's need the land very badly and they've got planning permission to develop the whole area, so the property's become pretty valuable.'

'And you've refused it?' Peter said, awed.

'Certainly not, I accepted it at once, before they could change their minds,' Dan answered. 'That's why I'm worth murdering. I'm really quite rich.'

'How many people know about this?'

'Helen, of course, Walter—oh, all of them, though they don't know what I mean to do with the money. I haven't told anyone my actual plans except Anna. Anna's a dear friend of mine and absolutely to be trusted.'

'What *are* your plans?' Peter asked.

'Why, to buy a house in the Highlands. Somewhere really solitary. Grey Gables, of course, is ruined, now that it's going to be surrounded by factories and council houses and houses for what I believe are called executives. They all have at least two bathrooms and two garages and a sun-parlour and a patio. It's bad enough here already and when they build up Danby's property we'll have no privacy left at all. So I thought of the Highlands, or something on one of the Islands, with acres of moorland round it on which, incidentally, no one will be allowed to shoot any living thing. And my idea is—it's a splendid idea really, if I can persuade Anna to agree—that she should come along as châtelaine. Forgive the fancy word, but I mean something rather superior to a housekeeper.'

'I don't think she'd take much persuading,' Peter said. 'But what about Helen? How is she going to take to this idea?'

'She may not want to come. I'll tell you

something, I don't think she's ever cared for our life at Grey Gables. I'll go further and say I don't think she's ever cared very much for me. I was just someone to cling to when she was badly hurt and helpless. Then she met Walter, a man who's actually weaker than she is, yet with a streak of cruelty in him that she enjoys. And he has no very deep love for his wife, so Helen may be able to arrange her life as she wants. I'll provide for her, of course. There may not be much money over when I've bought what I want, but she'll be able to afford a flat in London, or whatever it is she fancies.'

'You'll provide for her even if it turns out she's the one who's been feeding you poison?'

Peter saw a flash of something like despair in Dan Braile's eyes.

'Wouldn't it be as good a way as any of making sure she doesn't try again?'

'So you've some suspicions of her after all. You aren't certain it's Gina.'

Dan sighed. 'The truth is, I'm not certain of anything. I thought I'd made that clear. But Gina will not be admitted to my new house. I've had all I can stand of that young woman. And as a close friend of Gina's, my dear Peter, I'm afraid you won't be welcome either.'

'After that,' Peter said, 'it doesn't sound as if there's anything more for us to say to one another.'

He yawned deeply and got up. Strolling to the door, he looked out into the passage. Then he wished that he had not done this, for just then two men, carrying a covered stretcher, were edging their way round the bend in the stairs.

He turned back into the room. In a way it surprised him how little anger he felt with Dan. The man had suffered more than enough already.

'They're taking him away,' he said. 'I wonder if he's got any family. A wife. Children. He hardly spoke about himself.'

'He wasn't married,' Dan said. 'He lived with his parents.'

'Then I suppose they'll have been informed. They'll have to come down to identify him.'

'Yes. Peter—' Dan's tone had become conciliatory, as if he regretted what he had said the moment before. 'You saw a little of him. What was he like?'

'Likeable, I think. Intelligent. But he didn't seem to have found any direction in his life yet. I think he would probably have wasted it somehow or other.'

'But not as pointlessly as this. I suppose he was killed because someone waiting for me in that room thought it was I who'd just come in.'

'D'you know, I don't feel at all sure about that,' Peter said. 'I think it could have been the other way round.'

'I don't understand.'

'I'm sorry, I'm afraid I can't put it really clearly. It's just a vague idea, you know. There probably isn't anything in it. But I thought the reason Rolfe was killed might be that he wasn't you.'

The door swung open. Gina darted in, went straight into Peter's arms and clung to him. He could feel her trembling.

'What is it—what's happened?' she asked wildly. 'All the police—have they found him? Is he here? Is he dead?'

Then over Peter's shoulder she saw Dan.

She gave a short, shrill scream.

CHAPTER XI

Dan smiled. It was the small, controlled smile that never reached his eyes.

'I'm not a ghost,' he said. 'You have no need to fear me.'

She looked into Peter's face, still clinging to him.

'What are the police doing here?' She was almost whispering and her eyes were full of dread.

'There's been an—' He had almost said that there had been an accident, but there was no virtue in saying anything so untrue. 'It's Rolfe,' he said. 'He's been shot. You may as well know it now as later. I'm afraid he's dead.'

He did not know how she would take it. He had had the feeling earlier that she and Rolfe had begun to feel drawn to one another. He had even wondered, he remembered, if perhaps they had known one another already.

Her face went blank. It showed shock, but not much else, unless there was a trace of fear in the wide, strange eyes near his own. But many people feel fear at the mere mention of death, let alone sudden and violent death happening close to them.

She drew away from Peter, looking at Dan.

'What are you doing here?' she asked.

'What are you?' he countered. 'Why have you come alone? Are you an emissary, sent by that crew over there, to find out if my corpse had been discovered, or had you reasons of your own for slipping over secretly?'

His dislike of the girl could be heard in his voice, hard-edged and sarcastic.

'There was nothing secret about it,' she said. 'Alice Thorpe woke me and told me there seemed to be something strange happening over here and suggested I should come to see what it was. So I came, that's all. And when I got up to the house I saw the police cars and all the police about and an ambulance, so naturally I thought... Well, you could have been dead, vanishing the way you did. Of course that's what I thought.' She turned back to Peter. 'Why Adrian? What's he done to anybody?'

Dan answered, 'Your friend Peter and I disagree about why he was killed. I'm inclined to think it was because he was mistaken in the darkness for me. Someone who'd been slowly poisoning me lost patience and decided to make a quick job of it. It happened, you see, in the room where I'd been sleeping. But Peter thinks he was shot because he wasn't me. I find that enigmatic. I don't pretend to understand it.'

'Nor do I,' Gina said. 'What do you mean, Peter?'

He shook his head. 'I'm probably wrong, anyway. Gina, when did you go to bed?'

'To bed? Why? What does that matter?'

'You said Miss Thorpe woke you up, so you were asleep when the police came here, weren't you?'

'Yes, I went to bed straight away when

you and Adrian dropped me off at the house and I went to sleep almost at once, I was so tired.'

'What about the others? Do you know when they went to bed? You see, when I got up about two o'clock because I'd suddenly thought I might find Dan somewhere in the hotel, a lot of lights were on at Grey Gables. But when I looked out again some time after the police had got here they'd all been turned off. Did someone stay up, like last night, d'you know, in case Dan came back, and if so, who was it?'

'I don't know anything about it,' Gina said. 'I just looked into the sitting-room for a moment when I got back and there they all were, the Weldons and the Patons and Kate, playing cards—rummy, I think it was—and Alice Thorpe knitting as usual. And of course all the lights were on. But when she woke me the house was dark and everyone had gone to bed, but I don't know when they went. I think she'd gone to bed herself because she was in a dressing-gown, but I know she often prowls about the house at night because she never sleeps much, so I suppose that's how she saw the police cars come.'

'One wonders why she chose you to come and investigate,' Dan said.

'Why shouldn't she?' Gina asked.

'Shall we stop fencing with one another?' he suggested. 'I know, and you know I know, my dear child, that you've been trying to poison me. So I can understand that it would be important to you, when you saw the police cars over here, to find out if my body had been discovered. Naturally you came over as fast as you could. But why bring in Alice? Why say she woke you up? Isn't it the truth that you met her wandering around in the dark, as she often does, and that it was you who pointed out to her and not the other way round, that there were strange things happening here that you ought to investigate? Aren't you counting on her getting muddled when she's questioned and saying she's sure you must be right, whatever you've been saying?'

Gina stared at him in silence. The fear was back in her eyes, making her look more than ever like a startled child, scared in the threatening world of adults. Dan returned the stare with an expression almost of satisfaction on his drawn face.

At last she said in a low voice, 'He hates me. I've always thought how I hated him, but I've never thought how much he hated me. How stupid of me.'

'These things are seldom one-sided,' Dan observed. 'I have not enjoyed being poisoned.'

'But you know perfectly well I didn't do it.' There was wonder and defiance in her voice. 'Didn't I keep trying to get you to see a doctor?'

'Which is how you betrayed yourself,' he said. 'I'm afraid you're just not quite clever enough for what you attempted. You needed some doctor like that ass Barrow to come and see me, to avoid a post-mortem.'

She went a step nearer to him.

'And do you think I murdered Adrian?'

'It seems to me not impossible.'

She turned to Peter. 'Is that what you think too?'

273

'No,' he said. 'And neither does Dan. In his heart he believes your mother's guilty.'

'But there's a wonderful case against me,' Gina said.

'Peter doesn't think as I do,' Dan said, 'because he's at least half in love with you. A pity. The age difference is rather significant.'

'He isn't in love with me,' she said.

'Ah, but he is.'

'No.'

'Stop it, Dan,' Peter said. 'Stop torturing her. You know she's innocent.'

'You don't agree with my reasoning?' Dan said with lifted eyebrows.

Peter was bitterly angry, but his answer was quiet. 'In what you call your reasoning you've left out something important. As long as Gina was trying to make you see a doctor there was no need for anyone else to try.'

Dan's pallid face went empty for a moment, then astonishment showed on it.

'I never thought of that. Extraordinary.

So obvious, once you think of it.' He dropped his head into his hands. 'If I've been wrong, Gina—forgive me.'

The door swung open and Anna came in.

'There,' she said to Dan, 'they have done with me. There was nothing I could tell them, only that you came here that evening and I gave you a room and then took you home and of course about my cousin, the chemist. Now you come upstairs and rest. You have already done too much, you are looking worse. Later we go back to my house, but not now, the police say. They ask we stay here. So you come and lie down and I make you some tea.'

She took him by the arm and helped him to his feet.

Even that slight exertion made him breathe heavily. Leaning on her, he shuffled to the door. Peter held it open for him. Pausing there, Dan looked back at Gina.

'You never helped me to care for you,' he said. 'If you'd wanted me to, I should have loved you. Now all that I understand

275

fully about you is that I don't know you, I don't know you at all. I have perhaps been doing you a great wrong. Or I may not. Peter's logic goes farther than mine, but not far enough. Not nearly far enough for certainty. You may still be as guilty as I thought you.'

He went out with Anna's arm supporting him.

There was scorn on Gina's face. 'He can't admit he's wrong, can he? Can he seriously believe I murdered Adrian? *Shot* him? I don't know how to shoot. I haven't got a gun. I wouldn't know how to get one. You did say he was shot, didn't you?'

'Yes,' Peter said.

'Poor Adrian.' She went to the chair in which Dan had been sitting and dropped into it. 'Peter, you aren't in love with me, are you?'

'Let's not talk about that now,' he said.

'Yes, yes, we must. I never meant to talk about it at all, but now we must. After what he said. I know he's wrong.'

'Does it matter?'

'Of course it matters, because... Oh, I'd know if it was true, I'm sure I should, because I've been so in love with you ever since we met and I'm sure I'd know it if you felt anything about me at all. But you don't. Just now you're only embarrassed and afraid of hurting me. You needn't be, Peter. I've known all along this was something I'd have to go through by myself. I'll get over it, you know. People do, don't they?'

Her gaze locked with his as she made her declaration. Remembering Dan's warning that it would be a mistake to think of Gina as a child, that she was old beyond her years, Peter admitted to himself that over some things Dan had more perception than he had.

With a sad look she went on, 'Yesterday I almost believed it was beginning to happen. When you went to talk to Max and left me with Adrian, it was odd, it was as if we'd suddenly begun to understand one another. Yet I don't think we even liked each other much. There was just a feeling of something beginning...' Her voice shook. 'Peter, did Dan shoot him?'

'The police suggested that as a possibility,' Peter said, 'but they don't think so now.'

'But suppose he had a gun. He was in the war, you know. He may have managed to keep one all these years without anyone knowing. And he might have taken it with him to protect himself in case anyone came after him when he left home. And if Adrian came into his room in the middle of the night it would have frightened Dan and he might have shot at him before he even knew who it was.'

'No, it didn't happen like that,' Peter said. 'Dan left the hotel with Anna in the afternoon and Arthur helped. So they've both got alibis. Gina, about the gun, are you just guessing that perhaps Dan had one, or have you anything to go on?'

'I'm afraid I'm just guessing,' she answered.

'But if he had...' He paused.

'If he had and someone else knew of it,' she said, 'that person could have come over here with it to kill him.'

278

'Only I don't think that happened at all.'

'Why not?'

'For one thing, because of that game of cards you saw them all playing over there. I know when they went to bed. At least, I know when the lights were turned out, and it was after the police arrived. So it was after the murder. I think, when they're questioned, it'll turn out they've all got alibis as good as Dan's and Anna's.'

'I haven't.'

With a feeling of shock, Peter saw that the fear was back in her eyes. Also the defiance, a kind of angry courage. It made him want to take her in his arms and comfort her and before this evening he might have done it, but she had made that impossible now.

'Look, I may be quite wrong,' he said. 'One of them may have stayed up after the others went to bed and turned the lights out later. I wasn't thinking when I assumed they'd stayed together all that time.'

'Which of them?'

'How should I know?'

'I think, if I'd been coming over here to commit a murder, I'd have gone up to bed when all the others did and let all the lights be turned out, then I'd have slipped over here in the darkness. The last thing I'd have done would have been to leave the lights all blazing.'

'You're right, of course. So if they all claim to have been together playing cards until after two o'clock, we can be fairly sure they're lying. But it would have to be all of them, you see. Sticking together. And that would mean, wouldn't it, that they were in the whole thing together?'

'The poisoning too, you mean.'

'Yes, of course the poisoning.'

'My mother...'

'*If* they say they were all together. Though it's possible none of them had anything to do with the shooting.'

'But you're sure they had.'

'Not as sure as all that. We don't know anything about Rolfe. He may have been followed down here by some enemy of his own. He may even have come here in the first place to escape from someone. His murder may have had nothing whatever to do with Dan and the poisoning.'

She gave her head a slight shake. 'You don't believe that. Nor do I really. Perhaps I might if it hadn't happened in the room where Dan had been hiding. That's too much of a coincidence. Someone from over there came here and shot poor Adrian, thinking he was Dan. Only...' She wrinkled her forehead. 'You don't think that's what happened, do you? You said something about Adrian having been shot because he *wasn't* Dan. But you didn't explain it.'

'It's difficult to explain. Let's just say that if it had been Dan in that room, I don't think he'd have been shot.'

'So Adrian did have an enemy.'

'Perhaps.'

'I know you don't think so.' She stood up, raised her arms and stretched wearily. 'I'm terribly tired. Too tired to think. Peter, do you really believe my mother had anything to do with trying to poison Dan?'

He hesitated, wanting to say what would help her most. Uncertainly after a moment he said, 'I think I'd try to get used to the idea that perhaps she may have.'

'Oh, I'm used to it already,' she said. 'I haven't thought about much else for days. It's why I wanted you here, to have someone to hold on to if the worst happened. I never believed in cancer or an ulcer and I wanted a doctor because I thought if he started visiting Dan it might frighten off whoever was doing the job. It never dawned on me that might be just what the poisoner wanted.' Suddenly she came to him, slid her arms round his neck and pressed her mouth against his. Then she jerked swiftly away from him as if he had been trying to hold her against her will. 'I'm going now,' she said. 'That policeman can talk to me over there, if he wants to.'

Flinging the door open with such violence that it swung backwards and forwards behind her, she went running out.

Her embrace had a curious effect on

Peter. His nerves responded to it. He wanted to hold her back. At the same time his mind told him coolly that she was on her way to warn her mother, a murderess probably, at least by intention. But who could blame the girl for that?

He began to roam about the room, restlessly waiting for Crabtree to appear and tell him whether or not he was needed here. No one had actually instructed him to stay here until he was told that he could leave. Waiting for another few minutes, he suddenly made up his mind to go over to Grey Gables unless someone actually prevented his going.

Nobody did. A constable who was waiting at the foot of the stairs looked at him enquiringly and Peter told him where he was going. The man nodded and Peter went out into the dawn which was just breaking. Dull crimson clouds edged the horizon and trees and bushes which a little while before had been mere blurred shapes of blackness in the night were coming alive with dim green identities. It was very cold. Peter walked fast, seeing as soon as he emerged from the hotel that the lights in the house ahead had been turned on again. Gina had given the alarm already. The alarm for which someone perhaps had been waiting.

At the sound of his footsteps on the gravel of the drive the front door was opened. Kate stood there. She was in a dressing-gown but something about her gave Peter the impression that she had not been to bed. It was her hair, he realized. It was neatly brushed and it was not like her to think of giving it a brushing if she had been suddenly roused from her bed by the news of a murder. There were dark circles round her eyes and a look of extreme fatigue about her square-shouldered, sturdy body.

'Oh, I'm so glad you've come,' she said, closing the door behind him. 'I hoped you would. Gina's told us an extraordinary story. I don't know how much of it is true. She's very excited. I don't believe she knows that she's saying. She says Dan's in the hotel, but when Helen wanted to go straight over to him, she stopped her—literally physically stopped her—and said the police will be coming here any time now because there's been a murder. That young man, Adrian Rolfe. She said he's been shot. Surely it can't be true, Peter. And even if it is, it can't have anything to do with us.'

'It's true,' Peter answered, 'and whether or not it's got anything to do with you is something you know much more about than I do. Where are the others?'

'In the sitting-room. I think they've all come down. We were up pretty late, playing cards, still hoping Dan would show up. To think he was in that hotel all the time...I'll tell you something, Peter.' Her strong fingers grasped him by the arm. 'I think Max has been right about him all the time. He never liked Dan, you know. He didn't like my coming here. He always warned me I'd be disillusioned sooner or later. And I have been. If there's a thing I can't stand, it's cruelty, the sort of cruelty with which he's treated Helen. I never dreamt till it happened that he'd any cruelty in him. He always seemed to me so entirely gentle. I wish I could leave straight away, get the taste of it all out of my mouth, but of course that's impossible. I'll have to do what I can to help Helen. The Weldons aren't any use, they're both too damned selfish. And the Patons are too young and Alice Thorpe's too old... Come along now and tell the other's what's really happened.'

They were all in the sitting-room. All of them except Gina were in dressing-gowns. Gina was sitting beside Helen on a sofa with one of her mother's hands in hers. The bleak room as usual had a cold look, although it was really quite warm. The fire could not have had time to die down after everyone had gone to bed and someone had just added some fresh logs to it. Alice Thorpe was in her usual chair beside it, but for once was not knitting. The Patons for once were not entwined. Juliet Weldon was in a deep armchair with her head lolling back against it and her eyes closed. She might have been asleep except for the force with which her hands were grasping the arms of the chair. Walter Weldon was at the window, holding a curtain aside, looking out. As Peter came in he let the curtain fall and turned back to the room.

'If what Gina's told us about Dan is true,' he said, 'I shall feel I've wasted my life. I created that man. I worked to make him what he is. I helped him. I taught him. I built him up. Without me he'd have stayed in the obscurity where I wish to God I'd left him.'

'You overestimate your importance,' Kate said coldly. 'Dan's talent was always entirely his own. If you hadn't discovered it, someone else would have. His character is another matter. But this isn't the time to discuss that. You all want to know what's happened at the Manor House. Peter can tell us.'

Juliet spoke without opening her eyes. 'Do we want to know?'

'Of course we do,' Kate said. 'We want to know if what Gina's told us is substantially accurate.'

'All I want to know,' Walter said, 'is why Dan's treated us as he has. What have we done to deserve it?'

'Murder is of so little consequence,' Juliet murmured.

Kate turned on her angrily. 'Don't overdo it, Juliet. You're as anxious as the rest of us to know what happened.'

'I've told you what happened!' Gina cried out. 'Peter, tell them! They don't seem to believe me, or they don't want to. Tell them how you went looking for Dan and found Adrian's body, and how Dan came back with Anna and—and everything else.'

'I can tell them what Dan and Anna have told me,' Peter answered. 'I had a long talk with each of them and I may as well tell you that the problem of whether or not Dan's been poisoned or has been imagining it is about to be solved fairly soon. Specimens of his excreta have been sent to a chemist cousin of Anna's for analysis and he'll be able to supply the answer. Apart from that, the police are likely to insist on an investigation. I don't know whether or not Dan would have told them about his suspicions, but they knew of them from a letter he'd written to Rolfe, which they found in his wallet, so Dan could hardly deny them. In that letter, for not very logical reasons, he accused Gina of being the poisoner, but I doubt if he believes that himself any more. I think the suspicions of the police are going to be directed at the rest of you. Perhaps all of you. The best sense that I can make of what's happened is that you've all been in it together.'

'What, *us?*' the two Patons exclaimed.

'Oh dear, oh dear,' Alice Thorpe said, 'and I was doing my very best to protect him. Am I really to blame somehow?'

'I'm sorry,' Peter said. 'I didn't mean you, Miss Thorpe. Or you,' he added to the Patons. 'I don't think you're close enough to Dan to have been involved. But I think Dan's old friends had come to the conclusion that it was time to finish him off, before he could spend the hundred and sixty thousand he was going to be paid for Grey Gables on some remote place in the Highlands—'

'Peter!' Kate broke in, her face white with anger. 'Are you out of your mind?

289

Even if one of us—or two—' Her gaze dwelt briefly on Helen and then on Walter. 'Even if anyone here had a desire to kill him, why do you say *all* of us? Can you think of any possible motive I might have had for wanting to harm Dan?'

Peter crossed the room to the fireplace. He stood looking down into the flames for a moment, wondering how foolish he had been. The police would be arriving soon. This was a matter for them. But patience had never been one of his strong points. He turned to look at the tall old woman in the chair by the fire.

'Miss Thorpe, is it true that you overheard Kate Rowley and Gina discussing Dan's poisoning and that you warned him and that after that he ate nothing but the food you smuggled up to him?'

'Well, yes, it's true,' she said.

'How sure are you that it was Gina and not her mother?'

'D'you know, I've wondered about that myself,' she said. 'I thought it was Gina's voice, but I didn't actually look into the kitchen, because I didn't want them to see me and realize I'd overheard them. And Dan himself, when I told him, was certain it must have been Gina. And, to be on the safe side, I started to smuggle food up to him, and then the other evening I helped him get dressed and get away from here while everyone else was in the hotel.'

'Why, you old—!' Walter began.

'Walter!' Kate said sharply. 'Peter, I don't know why you've taken it into your head to believe the word of a semi-senile old woman rather than mine. After all, you and I have known each other for years now, haven't we? But you haven't answered my question. What possible motive could I have for wanting to harm Dan?'

'Well, if Helen and Walter had decided between them to poison him,' Peter said, 'and you'd found it out, I don't think I put it beyond you to demand a share of the spoils. And the same could be true of Juliet. That was Max's suggestion, incidentally—that she might settle for money because she was going to lose Walter anyhow. And you'd all be safe from betrayal because you were all involved.'

'It's lies, all lies!' Helen said suddenly, coming abruptly out of what had looked almost like a coma. 'Nobody's been poisoning Dan. The whole trouble is in his imagination.'

Juliet opened her eyes and looked at Helen with the cruel little smile on her lips that Peter had occasionally noticed before.

'It's a little late to be saying that,' she drawled. 'Let's not be fools. The poisoning will be proved as soon as Anna's cousin's done his job. And then we're all going to start accusing one another, aren't we? And why not? We've failed. One always tries to blame someone else for failure. I'm remembering just now how I warned you at the start that it wouldn't work. I made a brilliantly original remark. I said, "There's many a slip 'twixt the cup and the lip." That lovely cup of arsenic that Helen got through her poor old professor ex-husband and that we took it in turns to give to Dan. The funny thing is that when I said that I thought we were joking. Or did I already know we weren't? Or has it been a sort of joke all along, a wonderful joke that we'll be able to laugh over for the rest of our lives—such as they'll be?'

She began to laugh. At first it was only a quiet little giggle, but in a moment it had shot up into a high screaming sound, as it had the afternoon before in Dan's London flat. As she had then, she covered her face with her hands, the horrible sounds coming pouring out from between her fingers while her body shook all over.

Walter strode to her side, dragged her to her feet, snatched her hands away from her face and struck her sharply across it. She threw back her head and laughed louder than ever. He struck her again and she slumped suddenly against him and began to cry. He tossed her back into the chair with a look of loathing.

The Patons were looking on in horror. Turning to one another, they slipped into a close embrace and Rosie hid her face on her husband's shoulder.

He said sternly, 'While you're making these scenes, you seem to have forgotten that a murder's been committed. That's more important than attempted murder, isn't it?'

'The police are liable to think so,' Peter said.

Juliet's collapse had not surprised him. He had half-expected it. She had always been the weak link in the chain, far weaker than Helen, who, if she had not half Juliet's intelligence, had a quiet, unshakable stubbornness. In the face of overwhelming evidence and however much pressure was put upon her, she would probably cling to it that Dan's illness had been imaginary. But very little pressure on Juliet had made her betray the whole conspiracy. Her motives were too mixed for her to be reliable. She might even want revenge on Walter and Helen more than she wanted money or safety.

'Well,' Cliff Paton went on, 'why aren't you asking us for our alibis? Isn't that the most urgent thing at the moment?'

'I was thinking of leaving that to the police,' Peter said. 'It isn't really any business of mine.'

'But for our own peace of mind,' Cliff said, 'don't you think we might all state where we were when the murder happened? Do they know when that was?'

'It was probably about two o'clock,' Peter answered. 'When I found Rolfe only a little after that his body was quite warm and his blood hadn't started to congeal. And there's a possibility that it was the sound of the shot that wakened me.'

'In that case,' Cliff said, 'you can rule us all out, because we stayed up playing cards until well after two. Then we got tired of waiting. We decided there wasn't a chance of Dan showing up and we went to bed.'

'Except for Gina,' Walter said, his eyes becoming suddenly brighter. 'And of course Alice. They'd both gone to bed. However, it's difficult to imagine Alice carrying out a murder by herself. But Gina—what about her?'

'No!' Helen cried, taking a tight hold of the hand with which Gina was still covering one of hers. 'There's to be no dragging of Gina into this. It's bad enough that Dan should have suspected her. If I'd known it I'd have put a stop to it. I would—don't look at me in that surprised way, Walter! Gina's the one person I'd never have allowed to suffer for what I'd done.'

'Helen!' Walter said threateningly.

She rose to her feet, curiously regal in her old quilted dressing-gown.

'You are not to try to shuffle any blame off on to Gina,' she said. 'Anyway, you don't need to. As Cliff said, the rest of us were playing cards until well after two. We're in no danger.'

'Do you often play cards?' Peter asked. 'Is that how you usually spend your evenings?'

'Hardly ever,' Kate said. 'And if you're going to ask who suggested it last night, it was my idea. I tried to read but found I couldn't keep my mind on it, then I noticed it was more or less the same with everyone else, so I suggested we should play rummy and everyone jumped at it. Is that suspicious behaviour? Are you going to build something on it?'

'And not one of you left the room even for a little while?' Peter asked, directing the question at Cliff.

'Oh, I think we all did at different times,' Cliff said, 'but not for nearly long enough to cut over to the Manor House, do a murder and come back again. That would have needed a minimum of a quarter of an hour, I'd say, and certainly no one was gone for as long as that.'

'I'm curious about what made you stop playing,' Peter said. 'If you'd kept it up till two o'clock, why not till three?'

'Cliff told you, we just got tired,' Walter said. 'Speaking for myself, I was very tired. I'd been up all the night before, waiting for Dan, and I was longing to get to bed. I think I suggested some time earlier that we should stop.'

'It's true, he did,' Rosie Paton said. She had raised her head from Cliff's shoulder and looked interested, puzzled and rather frightened. 'And Kate got up and went to the window and lifted the curtain aside and said, "It's very dark." I remember that clearly. She said, "It's very dark."

Then we went on playing. And after a bit Kate went to the window again and said, "I don't know about the rest of you, but I'm going to bed." So we all agreed we wanted to go to bed and we broke up and went to our rooms.'

'And nobody but Kate looked out?' Peter said.

'I did,' Cliff said. 'I drew back our bedroom curtains before Rosie and I got into bed, but our room's at the back of the house so we shouldn't have seen whether the police had arrived or not. I suppose that's what you're wondering about.'

'Well, Kate,' Peter said, 'had the police arrived when you decided to stop playing cards?'

She did not answer. She looked thoughtfully round the room, as if she were making some private assessment of the people there, then she walked to the window and, as Rosie had just described it, held one curtain aside.

It was daylight outside. Seeing it, she pulled both the long curtains back. The light that came in through the window

298

made the light in the room look sickly. Walter switched it off. Kate remained at the window.

'The police are coming here now,' she said.

Gina stood up and went to Peter's side.

'What's going to happen?' she whispered to him.

'I don't know any more than you do,' he answered.

'Are they going to arrest anyone?'

'I don't know.'

'But you seem to know—something.'

'I'm not sure that I do.'

'Can you manage to forget those things I said to you over there?'

'I don't think I'll ever want to forget them.'

'Please try. I was very stupid. It wasn't fair to you. And now—now I'm frightened, because it's true, isn't it, I'm the only one without any alibi?'

He put an arm round her shoulders, steadying her.

'The police aren't fools,' he said. 'Tell

them everything you know and trust that things will work out.'

The front-door bell jangled. Its clangour started up echoes in the silent house, so that the noise of it seemed to go on and on.

As if for once it had occurred to Helen that she was mistress of the house, she went to open the door. After a moment she returned with Superintendent Crabtree and Sergeant Woodbury.

The superintendent looked round the room.

'It looks as if I needn't tell you why I'm here,' he said. 'Mr Harkness will have told you what happened over at the hotel. There are some questions I must ask you because certain accusations have been made. Concerning poison. None of you, of course, will be compelled to answer. Meanwhile, it may interest you to know that the boy Arthur has confessed to the shooting of Adrian Rolfe.'

CHAPTER XII

'Of course no one believed the boy's confession for a moment,' Max Rowley said a few days later, as he and Peter sat in the lounge of the Swan Hotel in Sisslebridge after the inquest on Adrian Rolfe.

Max had come down for it and had sat beside Kate. The verdict at the inquest had been murder against person or persons unknown. Rolfe's parents had been there and had given evidence of identification. They were a grief-stricken and bewildered but dignified pair who had denied that their son had ever had any enemies. The people from Grey Gables had hardly been questioned. Their massive alibi had protected them. But except for Gina, who had been allowed to return to her father, they had been told for the present to remain in the neighbourhood. Whether or not a charge was to be brought against any or all of them for the attempted murder of Daniel Braile was something that the police were keeping to themselves. Dan had been at the inquest, sitting beside Anna, avoiding even an exchange of glances with Helen and answering in a low weak voice the few questions that were put to him.

It was known that he had been given arsenic. That much had been established. But Juliet had refused to repeat, although she had not withdrawn, the confession and the wild accusations that she had hurled at her friends in the earlier hours of the morning before the police had arrived. Walter had claimed that she had not been herself at the time, which in a sense was true, and had said that she had been more than a little drunk, because all the time that they had been playing cards they had been drinking brandy. He insisted that she had lost her head and was stubbornly silent now only because she could not remember clearly what she had said.

Max had tried to persuade Kate to stay with him at the Swan, but she had replied that she must stand by Helen and had tried to persuade him to join her at Grey Gables, but he had as firmly refused.

'I can't stand that place,' he had said to Peter, who had moved into the Swan as builders had moved into the Manor House Hotel and had begun a large-scale operation of hammering and battering in all parts of the building at once, accompanied by music from half a dozen transistors, all blaring away so loudly that the men could enjoy the wailing music they craved above all the other noises they were making. 'I never could stand it. I like my comforts.'

The Swan was as comfortable as Anna had told Peter. It was an old building with beams in the ceilings, steps in unexpected places and uneven floors, but there was a plentiful supply of private bathrooms and it was cheerfully and comfortably furnished, well warmed and provided excellent food. The lounge in which Peter and Max were sitting had a good log fire burning in the old fireplace. They had chosen chairs near to it and were drinking coffee there after

303

the very good dinner that they had eaten.

'No one believed poor Arthur,' Peter said. 'He was very disappointed. No one's ever taken enough notice of him in his wretched little life. Anna was about the only person who bothered to be kind to him. But he thought that for once in his life he'd a sure-fire way of attracting attention.'

'I'm interested in Anna,' Max said, stirring sugar into his coffee. 'Have you ever given a passing thought to the fact that she might have had a motive for murdering Rolfe?'

'Anna? Impossible!' Peter said. 'What had she to gain? Besides, she'd an alibi. She was with Dan at Burley's End.'

'Was she, I wonder.' Max sipped his coffee. 'She'd a bicycle, hadn't she? That was mentioned at the inquest. She said it was her usual way of getting to work. So mightn't she have done the murder and gone hell for leather home again and been back there by the time you telephoned? Dan was in bed asleep, she said, and probably wouldn't have known if she was

304

in the cottage or not.'

'But what had she to gain?' Peter repeated.

'Well, it seems to me she's the one person who gains quite a lot as the result of the whole affair,' Max said. 'She worships Dan and now she's got him in her clutches. She seems to be the one person he trusts. And when he buys his estate in the Highlands, she's to look after him. That must be much more attractive than being housekeeper in a working men's club. Who knows, perhaps the two of them may even get married some time.'

'You're talking only about the murder of Rolfe then, are you?' Peter said. 'You don't think it's connected with the poisoning, because of course Anna had no way of tampering with Dan's food so long as he was at Grey Gables.'

'Just so,' Max said. 'There's no reason, really, why the two things should be connected. If by any chance it was Anna who killed Rolfe, she was just making use of an opportunity that chance thrust in her way.'

'But what was in it for her? You still haven't answered that. In what way could Rolfe have upset the beautiful plan of going away with Dan to the Highlands? How could he be a threat to her?'

'I should have thought he could have been a considerable threat.'

Peter shook his head. 'I don't see it.'

'Well, he was another disciple of Dan's, wasn't he?' Max went on. 'Mightn't Anna, with reason, have been afraid that he'd come between her and Dan? He was charming, wasn't he, and rich? He might have taken Dan right away from her to recuperate in luxury and perhaps she'd never have got him back again.'

'Luxury never meant much to Dan,' Peter said.

'Perhaps not when he was well, but illness changes people.'

'No,' Peter said, 'I'm afraid I don't find it at all convincing.'

'What do you think happened, then?'

'I know what happened. The question is whether I should talk about it.'

Max raised his eyebrows. 'Do you really

mean that, Peter? Do you really think you know?'

Peter nodded. 'And a lot of other people know,' he said. 'They know a lot more about it than I do. And one of them—Juliet—is going to crack and tell it all. I've seen her crack twice already and I know she'll do it again as soon as the police start putting pressure on her. She wants to tell it all, you know. The burden of her hatred of Helen is too much for her.'

'So you're sure the shooting and the poisoning are connected,' Max said.

'Of course they are.'

'Then either you believe Rolfe was shot by Gina or Alice Thorpe, or else you don't believe in the alibi of that card game. You think someone did leave it and that they're all lying when they said no one did. That includes the Patons, remember. They can't be as innocent as they seem if they're lying to support the others.'

'Suppose we forget about alibis for the moment,' Peter said, 'and think about motive. Three possible motives for Rolfe's murder have been suggested. The most obvious one is that he was killed in mistake for Dan, and that at first sight would imply that it was done by someone involved in the poisoning. But think that over. Would any of them really have wanted Dan killed like that? Wouldn't his body, full of arsenic, have been the most dangerously incriminating piece of evidence against them that could possibly have been found? I think, once he'd escaped from them and was on the way to recovery, they'd either have hoped he'd go away, deciding not to bring charges against them, or else, if they didn't believe he'd do that, they have removed him somehow and disposed of his body where it wasn't likely to be found. So I don't care much for that motive for murdering Rolfe. The second possibility, which I expect the police are investigating, is that in spite of the belief of his parents that their darling son hadn't an enemy in the world, there may have been someone who hated him bitterly, a jealous woman, it might have been, who followed him down here and shot him.'

Max nodded. 'But my impression is

you don't like that motive any better than the last. What's the third motive you mentioned?'

A frown of indecision appeared on Peter's face. He looked down at his coffee cup and fiddled with his spoon.

'The third's my own idea,' he said. 'I haven't tried to convince anyone else of it.'

'Try it out on me then,' Max suggested.

'That might be rather a mistake.'

'Oh come, you know I can keep things to myself. I'm not a lawyer for nothing.'

'Yes, you'll keep this to yourself, I know that.' Peter's face was sombre. He seemed to take no pride in having a theory of his own and to take no pleasure in it. 'Do you remember the other evening, Max, before Kate telephoned, when you and I had been talking about violence and you said you'd like to know a criminal who'd committed a particularly atrocious crime?'

'If you're talking about Kate—'

'I'm not, I'm not,' Peter said. 'I'm talking about you, Max. How you must have been laughing to yourself when you said that. It was perfectly true, of course. You were deeply interested in the effect of crime on your own nature. Your well-balanced, unaggressive nature. Because you were already involved in the poisoning of Dan, weren't you? And poisoning's generally regarded as a peculiarly atrocious sort of crime. Truly cruel, truly treacherous, truly cold-blooded. That's probably how it struck you yourself and why it so appealed to you.'

Max sat so still that it was hard to be sure that he was breathing. A slight gleam of sweat appeared on his finely modelled face.

'Now listen—'

'You listen to me for once, Max. It's generally been the other way round, hasn't it? I've generally been the listener. But you'd better let me finish now. If Kate was involved in that poisoning, and Juliet's going to confirm that she was, it could hardly have been without your knowledge. Could Kate suddenly have acquired a considerable sum of money without your knowing of it and knowing where it came from? And if you and Kate were involved in the plot for the sake of the money you were going to get out of it, then we can understand that impregnable alibi for Rolfe's murder, can't we? Kate was keeping them all together, playing that ghastly game of cards, so that none of them could be suspected while you came down and disposed of Braile.'

Max did not flare up. He did not laugh either. He very seldom flared up or laughed, Peter remembered. Max took most things coolly, treading warily, thinking before he spoke.

'So we've got back to Rolfe at last,' he said after a moment. 'You still haven't told me what you believe the motive was for his murder. Did I kill him for no reason at all?'

'I think you killed him because he wasn't Dan,' Peter answered. 'I think after we'd had our talk, when I came to you for advice after I'd been to Dan's flat, you must have come very quickly to the conclusion, as Rolfe did too and I did later in the night, that Dan was holed up in the Manor House Hotel. And you decided he'd got to be got away from there immediately, but got away alive, so that his body, full of arsenic, shouldn't be discovered. I don't know what you intended to do with him when you'd got him away, which you were going to do at the point of a gun. Shoot him and bury him somewhere a long way off, I suppose, or sink him in some convenient marsh or pool. It would have meant that Helen wouldn't have been able to sell Grey Gables at once. There'd have been some delay. But she'd have got the money in the end and you'd have had your share-out.'

'But none of this happened,' Max said in a voice quieter and more restrained than ever. 'And you haven't explained what you meant when you said Rolfe was killed because he wasn't Dan. You don't seem able to stick to the point.'

'I'm getting around to it,' Peter said. 'Incidentally, how you must have enjoyed yourself when I came to you and you analysed everyone's possible motive for the poisoning. Everyone's except Kate's and your own. And all quite accurately. You must have felt a wonderfully subtle pleasure in doing that. Well, afterwards, when I'd left you and you'd made up your mind Dan was hiding in the hotel, where you knew, from what I'd told you, that anyone could come and go without anyone noticing, you must have telephoned Kate and told her to keep everyone together for the evening because you were going to remove Dan and get rid of him. But what you didn't know was that Dan had already left the hotel with Anna and that Rolfe was going to hunt for him. When he and I said good night he didn't stay long in his room. He went looking for Dan and he found the room he'd been staying in easily enough. And he waited there because he thought Dan was coming back. He'd forgotten his beret when he left. It was on the dressing-table. There were some books there too and some newspapers. The place didn't look abandoned. So Rolfe lay down on the bed and waited. And at last someone came in. But it wasn't Dan, it was you, carrying a gun. I don't suppose either you or Rolfe knew who the other was, but Rolfe must have seen that whoever you were, you'd come looking for Dan in a murderous mood. And you must have seen that you couldn't afford to let this stranger live, now that he'd seen you and could later connect you with Kate. So you shot him and left. And Kate, frightened and restless because she didn't know what was happening, couldn't resist going to the window a couple of times to see if she could see anything. And the second time she saw a lot of police cars, so she knew that something had gone wrong and she broke the game up and sent everyone off to bed. And you, I suppose, went back to London. Well, there you are, that's my case.'

Max drank some coffee. His hand, holding the cup, Peter noticed, was not quite steady, but his voice, when he spoke, was as level as usual.

'I notice you've chosen a very public place for this conversation.'

'Wouldn't you, in my place?' Peter said.

'You wouldn't have dared say all these things if we'd been alone.'

'Naturally not. You may not have thrown that gun away yet.'

'I can't help wondering why you've said them now.'

Peter himself was not sure. A good deal of the drive to speak had been curiosity, to see how Max, who in so many ways had dominated him for so long, would take this rebellion. Even now Peter could not help admiring Max's calm, his careful weighing of his chances before he committed himself to any course of action.

'Well, we're old friends,' Peter said. 'We've talked about a lot of things in our time.'

'You mean you're giving me a chance to get away.'

'Not really. I almost wish I were. I don't like playing Fate. You'll realize, of course, that you've probably a better chance staying at home and denying everything than if you bolt. The police could pick you up quite easily.'

'If they thought it worth their while.

There's nothing in what you've said for them to take hold of.'

'Except, as I told you, that Juliet will crack. And it won't take long. She's longing to tell them everything and she will as soon as she finds the courage.'

There was a pause. Then Max stood up.

'This conversation never happened,' he said. 'I advise you to accept that for your own peace of mind. I'm going home now. I'll leave word with the police where to find me. Whether or not they find me there when they want me—well, I must think that over. Meanwhile, goodbye, Peter.'

'Goodbye, Max.'

Neat and precise but astonishingly swift-moving, Max left the room.

Peter stayed where he was, lying back in his chair, staring up at the beamed ceiling and hardly moving for almost half an hour. His coffee grew cold. His thoughts were a curious blank. It surprised him vaguely that he felt no anger with Max. His feelings seemed to have gone beyond anger. Perhaps, he thought, true anger requires a kind of innocence, and he had lost it. Whether he had done right or wrong in talking as he had he did not much care, but he knew that he wanted, almost with pain, to tear himself away from the whole situation, to return to a world where sane values operated and where you could count on finding goodness behind the face of apparent friendship.

At last he got up, went to one of the telephones in the hotel and dialled Caroline's number.

It was with intense relief and a sudden beating of the heart of a kind that he had not felt for longer than he had realized, that he heard the ringing stop and her voice replying.

The publishers hope that this book has given you enjoyable reading. Large Print Books are especially designed to be as easy to see and hold as possible. If you wish a complete list of our books, please ask at your local library or write directly to: Magna Large Print Books, Long Preston, North Yorkshire, BD23 4ND, England.

This Large Print Book for the Partially sighted, who cannot read normal print, is published under the auspices of

THE ULVERSCROFT FOUNDATION